Worth the Effort
(A Better Way)

by

Larry Ruegg

TO: Future Passengers of the "Douro Spirit" — ENJOY THE CRUISE! ENJOY MY FIRST NOVEL!

Larry Ruegg 8/18/14

larryruegg@gmail.com

DORRANCE PUBLISHING CO., INC.
PITTSBURGH, PENNSYLVANIA 15222

Dorrance Publishing Co., Inc.
701 Smithfield Street
Pittsburgh, PA 15222
Visit our website at *www.dorrancebookstore.com*

ISBN: 978-1-4809-0238-1
eISBN: 978-1-4809-0531-3

Prologue: "A Big Apple"

It was a beautiful, fall afternoon in New York City. At least one person was enjoying his walk from his hotel, but the others in the mass of people were simply rushing like they were late for work. The sun was shining, but the air was cool as a breeze swept in from the ocean across the cooler water. For that reason, he wore a sweater, but not a hat. He walked at a leisurely pace, but his heart pumped faster than normal because of what was to happen that night.

He and his wife talked about it. Neither looked forward to what was going to take place, but it was now unavoidable. Matters had advanced too quickly, and both were too surprised at the turn of events. They had little time to plan for this, and now it was here. They had no idea of what would happen, because the odds were yet highly against them. Basically, their emotions were shredded about the entire thing. But, it must be faced. There was no longer any possibility of getting out of it now. Ward's mind shifted back and forth from fear to hope, and there was no way of changing that.

Ward Adamson was fifty-seven years old but kept himself in good shape. He didn't have much choice with that, because his wife was a nurse and made certain he kept up with a healthy regime. He laughed to himself as he thought about it, but knew his wife had been most helpful, much more than if he had simply done it by himself. They had been in New York several times before today, but tonight would be very different. Over the years he had come for pleasure or for meetings related to his work. All of those times, he had arrived in the Big Apple with different expectations than what was whirling around in his mind right now. He had enjoyed the frequent visits for musicals and plays. He had never been nervous about the periodic meetings that his vocation required. But now his heart was beating faster, and his stomach seemed to be telling him that tonight there was a new game in town, and he was one of the players.

While he was not a fatalist—he did not believe that the journey of one's life was "woven, measured, and cut"—he yet thought about the strange things that had happened to him during his life so far. He particularly was centered on the immense changes during the past months. How could such a thing have happened to him, giving influence to the rest of his life?

He wondered about how things had changed so much during the past twelve months. Things had been comfortable for him for so many years, but one meeting with a friend had changed all of that, and what followed had radically and swiftly brought him to this point in his life. Tonight it could change even more, or it would be the beginning of the end of what had been interjected into his former life.

He looked around him, looked at the building. Madison Square Garden seemed bigger now than when he had attended an NBA game there a few years ago. He began to shake his head a little and wondered why and how he had gotten to this point. Everything had changed in the previous months, and there was no turning back at this point. He found an entrance and opened the door. A guard questioned him and checked everything before allowing him to go any further.

Once inside, Ward walked into the main arena and entered. He stopped for a minute, just to get an overall image of his surroundings. He looked over and up to where he had been seated for that basketball game, but now he was on the main floor. Then he slowly made his way to the stage. He began to walk at a slow pace because he wanted to absorb a "feeling" for the room itself before the events of that evening. He had come early for that reason—to become more comfortable with the room, the setting, the entire ambiance of where he would be tonight.

How could he ever have imagined he would be in this situation? What were the odds against it? He had studied for twenty-one years to prepare for his career, but after working thirty years it could all change now. Life has a way of dealing with its inhabitants: "the affairs of mice and men oft go astray."

Those thirty years had been a good experience. He had worked hard and done good work. He had been very faithful in his calling. He had helped many souls in their faith journey. The Reverend Ward Adamson thought about his past responsibilities as a parish pastor. Yet, those same experiences with people had led him to reconsider the direction of his remaining life's work. Such considerations were now on his mind as he reached the stage. Looking around the auditorium, he became a little tense as he thought about where he was and why he was there. All of this would be quite different for him.

Ward took a deep breath and tried to calm himself about what lay ahead for him this night and the days following. He saw his name on one of the podiums and slowly walked over to it, grabbing both sides as he reached it. He took another deep breath. "Well," he thought, "this will be the test." He surveyed the room again. He walked around the other nine podiums and read the names. Then he left the building and walked back to his hotel, but his mind was filled with a life story that had led him to this momentous event in his life. He wondered if it all was worth it.

BOOK ONE

Chapter 1:
"Once Upon A Time"

It had all started for Luke and Sara Adamson's young boy when he became active in the congregation's youth program. It wasn't so much the relationship with the other youths. That had been enjoyable because Ward was an extrovert and appreciated meeting new people. He found all of them to be interesting, as well as challenging. Every new acquaintance became a new learning experience. In addition, travel to Church Youth Conventions gave him some more opportunities to acquaint himself with ideas from people around the nation. But the greatest benefit came in discussions led by very intelligent and caring leaders in Faith Lutheran Church: the congregation of his youth in Milwaukee, Wisconsin.

Ward soon learned at an early age to think more critically and accurately about important issues concerning life, church, and society. Bob Schwartz, the Youth Advisor at his home congregation, once told him, "Don't just read or listen to words without considering the author's or speaker's agenda and motives. Give thought to what those words imply within the context of their setting. The English language has been deteriorating for many years due to politics and advertising—perhaps, even to laziness on the part of the people. All have put their own slant on what they write and speak."

"Why would they do such a thing?" the young Adamson questioned. "How is that even possible?"

"It is because too many people have never really learned English," Bob had responded. "We have lost most of the case forms of verbs and nouns because of laziness and misuse. Even words themselves have been used in ways far from their original intention. A simple example is that the noun 'cool' once only referred to a temperature. Another example is the misuse of 'I' and 'me' in a sentence. We seldom follow the traditional case forms in those and other words.

"Latin is a dead language, so it does not change. But, all of that language assists us with accuracy in speaking and writing, which we are now missing. Latin forms about sixty percent of our English vocabulary and language. Latin has various cases for nouns: nominative, genitive, dative, objective. Such differentiating assists us in language accuracy. Add to all of that the fact that we rarely ask a speaker: 'What do you mean by that word?' We simply assume that their understanding of any word is the same as our history and use of that particular word. That is not always the case, especially if we do not read and listen carefully."

"I understand that. In fact, I have had to rephrase my questions sometimes simply because the other person thought I meant something else."

"It can get even worse," the youth director responded. "For example, what do I mean by this statement: 'God loves Jim as much as me'?"

Ward thought a bit and then simply said, "When I think about it, I'm not certain. Do you mean to say that God loves Jim and me equally; or do you mean that God and I love Jim equally?"

"When I used the pronoun 'me' in that sentence, it says that God loves both Jim and me equally. If I wanted to say that God and I equally love Jim, the phrase should be: 'God loves Jim as much as I.' 'I' is a nominative case and 'me' is an objective case. Most often the confusion comes about when associated with the word 'like.' 'If you are like me...' Just add the word 'am' at the end, and the difference is obvious. 'If you are like me am...', when it should be 'If you are like I am...', which can be shortened to 'If you are like I...'"

"Of course," Ward responded. "That makes sense, and it also conveys accurately what the speaker wants to say."

Ward, as is true for all young people, was slowly being influenced—for better or for worse—by people he met, especially when he engaged in conversation with them.

Chapter 2:
"Love Makes the World Go 'Round"

Love—or, more correctly, infatuation—came to Ward the first day of high school. Lisa was beautiful and had a vibrant air about her. She was very friendly in spite of really being an introvert. They were assigned hall lockers next to each other and also adjoining chairs in home room because of the alphabetically arranged assignments. Her last name was Aaronson.

"Hi," Ward said with a smile. He spoke first because he was an extrovert. "My name is Ward, and I'm new here."

Lisa smiled and replied, "Hi, back! My name is Lisa. This is my first year, too."

The warning bell sounded and cut short their first conversation, but Ward promised himself they would continue it. Both parted and went in opposite directions to their first class, but met again at the second class. Ward saw she was already seated in the middle row, but two other girls sat on each side of her. It was Ward's first disappointment, but he did sit in the row behind her.

Little by little and day by day that first week, they met more often in school, both at their lockers, but also in a couple of classes. At those times, Ward tried to "hang back" until she entered the room. Then he would also try to sit next to her, although he was successful in that only twice that week.

Ward enjoyed the repartee in those times when they had a chance to talk but was somewhat timid about the thought of moving the relationship any deeper too soon. Even though he was an extrovert, he doubted he would be able to get up the nerve to ask her for a date to the upcoming school dance. His thoughts ran like this: "If I ask her to go with me and she says, 'No, I already have a date,' Or, 'No, I don't want to go,' I will be embarrassed." Therefore, their conversations were simply about "When did you move here? Where did you live before? Have you any brothers and sisters? What do your parents do? What do you like to do?"

Things looked a little more promising that first Sunday. Ward saw her entering his church with her parents. "Good morning, Lisa," came out with a smile, returned with a nod and a cute smile.

"Do you belong to this church, Ward?"

"All of my life," was his proud and happy response. "Well, technically—theologically—ever since I was baptized." This is great, he thought.

Lisa kept smiling and gave the introduction. "These are my parents, Andrew and Hilde Aaronson."

"I'm a classmate of Lisa's," Ward said as he shook the extended hands. "Our hall lockers in high school are next to each other."

During the short conversation that followed, he was informed that they were members of a similar church in their former city and just started visiting churches to learn where they would be comfortable again in a new congregation. Ward quickly interjected, "Lisa, we have a nice youth group here, and we meet tonight at seven. Why don't you come with me tonight? I know you would see quite a few of the people with whom you have classes at school."

That's all it took. Her parents agreed it would help Lisa become acquainted with a new group of her peers. That would ease the transition brought about moving to a new community. Ward's parents came over to them at that point and general introductions were again made. When they learned Lisa would visit the youth meeting that evening, both sets of parents made the necessary arrangements for transportation. Then, Ward's mother asked the Aaronsons to sit with them during worship. They would help them during the service. Afterward, the Adamsons would introduce them to others during the fellowship time. They wanted this new family to feel right at home in their church.

All went well that morning, and it was equally enjoyable for both Lisa and Ward during the evening youth meeting. Lisa was impressed and pleased with the group. She enjoyed getting acquainted with the others her age and was happy to be with Ward for a longer period of time away from school. She was especially impressed by the ability and congeniality of the Youth Director. It did not take much effort for her to convince her parents that this church should be the one they ought to join. Her parents agreed because they had felt the same kind of openness, friendliness, and quality in all they had experienced during the morning worship service. It was no surprise, then, when the pastor and another member of the congregation called and asked if they could visit them to discuss the congregation's mission. They would also answer any questions the new family had.

Following that visit, Lisa and family asked that arrangements be made to transfer their membership; and all was completed within a short time. Lisa attended the next youth meeting as a "member" and was again happy she had done so. The transition had been much easier than she had thought it would be. She had left many friends in her previous community and church, but she was happy with the change. Ward was extremely happy, also.

After the next youth meeting, Lisa and Ward were alone, waiting for transportation to their homes. The school dance was that coming Saturday, and Ward had debated with himself about asking Lisa to go to the dance with him. He did not want to disturb the beginning of a very nice friendship, but he also wanted to take Lisa to that dance. Finally, he thought of a way to ask her. He hoped it would lessen his anxiety about a possible refusal and rejection. It wasn't the best way, but it was the only way his shyness with Lisa would allow.

"Lisa, are you going to the school dance Saturday?"

"No," was the only response she gave.

"Why not?" Ward inquired with a timid voice.

There was what seemed to Ward to be a long hesitation, but—in reality—it was only a moment or two. "No one asked me," was Lisa's short answer.

"Then," an even more hopeful Ward slowly asked, "would you go to the dance with me?"

Lisa was somewhat surprised by the method of the invitation, but also amused by it. She had also hoped Ward would ask her, but she had been hesitant to raise the issue. Now, she pleasantly answered, "Yes!"

"God is good!" Ward thought to himself. Arrangements were again made for a group date and plans for providing transportation to and from the dance. That was the solid beginning of a life together. It also was the start of a variety of experiences—some, which very few people would ever have.

Chapter 3:
"Time Marches On"

Until that future experience happened, the years passed quickly for Ward and Lisa. During the remaining high school years, their affection for each other grew—as did their understanding of the ways of the world. That was especially true in terms of economics. The biblical "Love of money is the root of all evil" seemed an ever-present truth to explain most social ills. Thinking about such understanding of human immorality, there came to Ward the decision to study for the Lutheran, ordained ministry.

He and Lisa talked about it. Because both of them had been favorably exposed to church work, Lisa was very supportive of his preliminary choice. "It will mean eight years of school after high school, but I think you would be a very good pastor."

"Thanks for your support" was Ward's quick response. "Have you decided on a nursing career yet?" They had talked off and on about their individual dreams and futures. Unspoken had been any talk about their future together. The general understanding—even among their classmates and their own parents—was that Lisa and Ward were "going steady." But neither of them—especially Lisa—had brought up the idea of marriage. Lisa didn't, because she was somewhat "old fashioned" about such feminism. Ward—again, in spite of being an extravert—hesitated because he remained somewhat shy with Lisa.

"I think I would really like to become a nurse," Lisa answered. "I have looked into several programs but haven't made any definite decision yet. Being a doctor would also interest me, but I like people, and I just think nursing gives me a better chance to relate more closely to individuals."

"That sounds correct to me," Ward gave his support. "You are very good with people. That is only one of the things I love about you."

"You mean there are more things you love about me? I would like to know what they are." Those were unusual statements from Lisa, but she was trying to prompt Ward into being a little more "romantic." They had not progressed in their relationship as far as some of their classmates had in theirs, but "love talk" was not that common for either of them.

Ward was caught off guard. He was now on the spot, but he had to answer. "I guess that's a major item. Besides the fact you are one of the prettiest girls in school, is also that I have learned to trust you. I remember a video lecture I once viewed at church. It was about marriage. The author once asked his girlfriend, 'Will you marry me?' The girlfriend answered, 'But I don't know if I love you.' The author asked again, 'But, do you trust me?' She answered, 'Of course I trust you.' To that the author said, 'That will do for a beginning.'" That was also the beginning of talk about marriage between Lisa and Ward.

It was helped along by a discussion one night at the youth meeting. The Youth Director presented opening statements regarding various ideas about marriage, especially as they had developed in the United States. He noted that movies and "Romance Novels" presented the notion that people met, they got acquainted, they fell in love, they got married. He said he did not really agree with all of that. Asking how many had seen the video lecture about marriage they had used a few years ago, he asked them, "What did that author present as the most important element in marriage?"

Ward raised his hand, thankful he had recently talked with Lisa about it. "Trust in each other," he proudly stated.

"Correct," the leader responded. "It is trust with each other that is the major element in getting married. That is because true love does not come before marriage. That is just what some people call 'puppy love' and liking each other. We might even call it 'infatuation.' True love comes after marriage or the marriage will not last, because 'puppy love' is not enough to sustain such a relationship.

"I have been married only for five years. But, I love my wife much more now than when we first got married. And, if our love for each other does not continue to keep growing, our marriage will not last. Remember, that was the way it was in biblical times. Often the bride and groom hardly knew each other. Most of the times they did not pick out their own spouse; parents made the arrangements. The couple trusted their parents and began to trust their new spouse. It was that trust within the intimacy of a wedded relationship that their love developed and grew. True love grows out of trust and then continues as love increases."

Chapter 4:
"Getting To Know You"

After the discussion and the meeting ended, Ward and Lisa talked more about getting married than ever before. Their togetherness in school, church, and the community was making their shyness about the subject less of a problem. They easily talked about the coming change in their lives individually, and also the change in their relationship. That discussion continued during their remaining years in high school, especially during their solo dating as juniors and seniors. During their first two years they had always dated in a group. Now they began to talk about the possibility of their own marriage to each other. It was their frankness and trust in each other that permitted them to learn more deeply about each other.

They also talked about marriage in relation to the years of schooling ahead, especially for Ward. As they talked and discussed each one's dreams for the future, their love for each other deepened. They were mature enough to recognize the obstacles against getting married immediately after high school. It became obvious that it would be difficult for both of them to attend the same college. Lisa had found a nursing program where she could spend the first two years in a special nurses training. After that she could attend college with Ward in order to obtain a Master's Degree in Nursing, which would even allow her later on to teach nursing if she wished.

With that goal in mind, that fall Ward set off to Penn State University for his undergraduate studies after high school graduation. Lisa went to another school to begin becoming a nurse. Although their original intention had been to marry after college, they first had another of their serious—and mature—conversations. They both, reluctantly, agreed that it would be a good idea to try dating others in their respective schools. That made sense to them because neither had ever dated anyone else. Secretly, both were pessimistic about the results of such dating, but it was just another sign of their maturity at their young age. They talked to their parents about it and everyone agreed.

Those first two years passed quickly, punctuated by many conversations through computers. Both tried dating and found it enjoyable. But the greatest joy after each date was conversing with and seeing each other via computers. Both Lisa and Ward found their love toward each other grow and strengthen in their separation. Neither found respective dates of the same quality they had experienced in each other during the four years of high school.

During the summer vacation after those two years, Lisa confirmed her transfer to Penn State to be with Ward. She was enrolled in classes which, after two more years, would end with the awarding of a Master's Degree in Nursing. That meant she and Ward would graduate together, with Ward receiving his Bachelor of Arts Degree.

Chapter 5:
"Together Again"

Ward was just about to reach the sidewalk toward the social studies building when he saw Lisa coming from her dormitory. He waved at her as she approached and then waited for her. He was happy she had also decided to take this class with him. They had both gotten interested in politics in the United States; so, together, they had registered for a course in "The History of Politics." While Ward had planned on a double major of English/History, his Bachelor of Arts Degree required the more varied education provided by classes in a variety of educational disciplines. This social studies course filled the requirement. The same was also required for Lisa, now that she was working on her master's degree. Such varied exposure had long been a guiding principle of liberal arts education. Founders had decided generations ago that the population of any society needed people educated with a broad basis of learning and experience. Specialties could be studied afterwards in specific graduate schools—in Ward's case, it would be four years of seminary: two years of academics, then one year of internship, then a final year of academics.

"Ready for the start of your political career?" a smiling Ward joked when Lisa was near. "I have mixed feelings about this because I have always believed that a monarchy is the best form of government..." He waited for any response from Lisa, but received only a frown. Then he continued, "...if I could be king."

Lisa laughed with him. "Very funny. And I don't think I will ever have a political career; not unless the nursing profession won't have any jobs when I graduate."

"I'm certain you will be great at whatever you do," Ward replied as he gave her a quick kiss. "I just hope I will do as well at my work as you."

They both turned toward the building and walked hand in hand through the open door. Ward spoke again. "Anyway, with all the turmoil in our past and present politics, this should be an interesting class. And, I'm also happy you're taking it with me."

"Did I really have a choice?" Lisa's smile let him know she was kidding him. "You know I like being with you, especially after two years in a different school." Both of them felt the same. It had been difficult for them to have been in different schools. But now they had these two years together, with the added benefit of sharing some classes. Besides, they now had a chance for discussion with each other in their free time.

They were both surprised when they entered the lecture hall. It was almost time to begin, and they had expected there would be a large group. That was not the case. Ward, especially, had thought there would have been a lot of interest because of the turmoil during the first three decades of the twenty-first century; particularly where U.S. politics were concerned. Now he remembered what his grandfather had told him. Politics had become so terrible that there had been long periods of time when voters had decided all politics were corrupt—it did not seem to matter which party was in control. Even their church Youth Director had discussed with them stories similar to what Ward's grandfather had told him.

Ward's grandfather was of Norwegian descent and had visited relatives in Norway a few times. While there, the Norwegian relatives often talked with him about U.S. politics. All of them—as had been true of much of Europe in those days—knew a lot about what was going on in the United States. The same was not true the other way around. U.S. citizens knew little about government in "foreign" lands.

The Norwegian relatives had asked Ward's grandfather, "Why do you Americans put up with such politics?"

The grandfather answered the relative with a question: "Tell me, Knut, what percentage of Norwegians eligible to vote actually do cast a vote in your elections?"

Knut quickly had responded, "Between eighty and eighty-five percent."

Ward's grandfather then gave his answer, "In the U.S., we are very lucky to have forty to forty-five percent; often a lot less than that." To an astonished question of "Why?" the grandfather had continued, "I guess our voters just 'gave up.' They began to feel it didn't matter anymore. They were convinced nothing would change."

Ward's thoughts were interrupted by the entrance of the professor. "Welcome to the History of U.S. politics," he announced. "Or, maybe I should say, 'Welcome to the History of the Growth of Political Apathy.'"

After a brief, groaning laugh by those present, Professor Schneider continued. "The word 'politics' actually means 'of and for the people.' President Lincoln knew, as we read in the Gettysburg Address, '...that government of the people, by the people, and for the people shall not perish from the earth.'

"Well, we are very close to that disastrous happening. We have rapidly been approaching that time when the few elect the many to do whatever they want. It has grown to the point which fulfills the axiom that 'power corrupts and absolute power corrupts absolutely.'"

Ward whispered to Lisa, "I think I will like this class. He's not going to sugarcoat anything." Lisa gave a nodding smile of agreement and grabbed Ward's hand as Professor Schneider continued.

"We presently have a problem in getting people to vote. There is that apathy among many who claim it doesn't matter which party is in power because the majority of people find their situation getting worse with each administration. In addition, for several generations there has been the misconception that 'one vote doesn't make a difference.' The problem with that is when over fifty percent of the voters use the same excuse, it is not just one vote.

"The present voting system—theoretically—is set up so one vote could make a difference in a national election. It is highly improbable, but it is possible that one vote could determine a win at the lowest level, and a change there could move up the line and change the results in each level up to the top. I think it is the remoteness of that possibility that convinces people their vote will not change any final results.

"Those who examine such activities in our society have also heard from certain sources about another problem in voting. It has to do with voting in a Primary Election which has multiple candidates. For example, let's say there are ten people on the ballot. The voters must vote for only one. One person of those ten gets twenty-one percent and another person twenty percent and another nineteen percent and another eighteen percent down to the last. What happens is that only the top two persons might go on to another run-off election. Notice that the top two only received forty-one percent of the vote. Those two combined did not receive a majority of the votes cast. In truth, then, fifty-nine percent of the voters did not want either of the top two, but would be stuck with one of them.

"There have also been Party Primaries with more than two persons on the ballot. In our history, there once was a party election with four persons seeking the party nomination to run in the final election against other party candidates for election to the U.S. Senate. Only twenty percent of the voters actually voted, and the results were that the winner got thirty-four percent of the vote; second place got thirty-one percent and the remaining two shared the rest. That one winner got the nomination, even though sixty-four percent of the voters did not want him as the nominee. Add to that the fact that the winner only had thirty-four percent of the twenty percent who actually voted. In situations like that, the 'winner' might claim that he had 'mandate from the people,' but the actual number of people who voted for him was extremely small.

"In addition, all four of those candidates had simply announced they had chosen to be on the ballot and had the money to run a campaign. The voters had no 'say' in the start of this entire process. There is something extremely immoral in such a system.

"That is precisely what the investigators learned through many interviews. A majority of the voters did not care for the person who won that primary. However, with the present voting system, he remained the only choice.

"But, suppose the system was changed in this way. There are ten people on the ballot and each voter needs to choose 3—ranking them as first choice, second choice, and third choice. When the votes are counted, they are also given a ranking. First choice gets five points, second choice gets three points, and third choice gets one point. It would be the total points that would count. With that system, the final winner could be any one of the ten, even if they did not have the highest first choices. Such a method guarantees a vote which is closer to the wishes of the most voters.

"So, then, let's see how we got to this point."

The rest of the hour was spent with the professor presenting various situations and then showing how the original intention of each procedure began to disintegrate as politicians stretched each to their own advantage. Then there was time for questions from the class along with clarification by the professor. After that, he presented a new situation. And the same pattern was repeated, giving examples of how the entire electoral process and government itself had changed.

One of the situations the professor talked about was the example of President Harry Truman. It had to do with an article about the former president, particularly after he left office. The source of the article was unknown, so the professor read it as he had received it:

"Historians have written that the only asset (President Truman) had when he died was the house where he lived. His wife had inherited the house from her mother. When he retired from office in 1952, his income was a U.S. Army pension reported to have been $13,507.72 a year.

"After President Eisenhower was inaugurated, Harry and Bess Truman drove home to Missouri by themselves with no Secret Service following them.

"When offered corporate positions at large salaries, he declined, saying, 'You don't want me, you want the office of the President, and that doesn't belong to me. It belongs to the American people and it's not for sale...'"

That was an eye-opener for those attending and it brought about a frenzied discussion from the small class, led by a very pleased professor.

When the hour was over, Lisa and Ward stayed a little longer with a couple of questions. That evening they had a chance to talk further about it, surprised that the subject interested them so much. "Maybe we might have a chance to bring up further questions about the nature of political campaigns," was Ward's thought near the end of their discussion. "Let's think about it and write some things down so that we ask him before this term is over."

It was during a discussion about political campaigning that Ward raised his hand. When asked, Ward spoke. "I have noticed that, during these campaigns, politicians make extremely general promises. A problem comes about when they are elected, because all of their actions have to be more specific."

The professor smiled, thought a bit, and then nodded his head. "Hmmm. That is a great observation. In other words, 'Promises are made in general terms; actions are always in specifics.' Thank you. I will be adding that thought to my lectures. Are there any further comments on that observation?"

Several hands were raised, and the class agreed with Ward's comment. Lisa smiled at Ward and squeezed his hand with her approval. At the end of class, the professor asked Ward to remain. "Thank you, again, for that observation. If you haven't decided on a major yet, maybe you should think about politics."

"No, thank you. Long ago I planned on becoming a minister, and I think I am much better suited for that. There are a lot of vocations where a person needs to have a deceitful nature in order to be successful. I am not that kind of person now and hope I never change."

"Well, maybe our political system will eventually change."

"I won't hold my breath until that happens. But, thank you for the compliment—I think."

But the professor wasn't done with the discussion. "Ward, I don't think the politicians will do the changes that are needed. Each new one claims they will, but the system just destroys their good intentions. All of them begin to think they are immune, but slowly they all fall in to the pattern. I guess they believe that 'the end justifies the means,' so they keep making exceptions in their actions thinking that—in the end—they will be able to revert to their own intentions. That never happens.

"Some time ago, the voting record of each person in Congress was tracked. It was reported what percentage of votes by each was beneficial to the persons who contributed money to each one's political campaign. There were many where that percentage was around eighty percent. In other words, that kind of lobbying with financial support got bills passed which benefited those who contributed—up to eighty percent of the laws for which a lot of congressional members voted. That is simply unacceptable. It is immoral. It is despicable. But, it is what keeps in power those who are already in power."

Ward was smiling as he spoke. "That's because we become how we act. That is also why 'the end never justifies the means.' The means are the actions we do, and we become what we do. Therefore, such political change is very improbable."

"But, not impossible," was the professor's response. "That's why I emphasize the need for all eligible people to vote. The future of politics is in the hands of the people. If they want things to go on as poorly as before—and it will get worse—then it won't change. It is up to the people. The voters need to set the rules and not vote for anyone who will not comply."

"I agree," said Ward. "I just do not see that happening. People are so prejudiced by the present system that most do not recognize the faults. There are always better ways, and such change is always worth the effort, but—politically—people are lazy."

""Ward, you have a good head on your shoulders. I wish you well in whatever you do, and I am happy to have you in this class.

"You could do something to help a change. If you and Lisa would recommend this course to your friends so that more people become informed about our politics, it would help to 'get the word out.'"

Both Lisa and Ward tried speaking affirmatively at the same time. They laughed and then, individually, each spoke in the affirmative.

Chapter 6:
"To Love and To Cherish"

The last two years of college passed quickly, and both Lisa and Ward graduated with honors. Things were different by then, because Ward had officially proposed to Lisa and much time was spent in planning the wedding. That wedding was held in August just before Ward had to move to Philadelphia to begin his seminary training. That schooling would last four years: three years of class work and one year of internship. Lisa obtained a nursing position in a hospital near their seminary apartment. She began what was jokingly called, "Working on her PHT Degree"—"Putting Hubby Through."

Their life together went very nicely, especially because they had prepared so well. After seminary, Ward was ordained and was called to be a pastor of a small church in Indianapolis, Indiana. Lisa continued her nursing career at a neighboring hospital, taking time off only to raise their children. Ward was very faithful in his parish work. God gave him a great deal of success in the rapid increase in the size of the congregation and its influence in the city. All went very well for thirty years. Then there was a very big and unexpected change.

BOOK TWO

Chapter 1:
"Nothing Is As Permanent As Change"

It had been a very wealthy, influential member of Ward's congregation who instigated the big change in Ward's and Lisa's future. Ward was in his own church office early, anxiously awaiting the arrival of Dennis Davies. He was wondering what it was about, because Dennis had seemed somewhat secretive when he made the appointment. All he had said was that it was very important.

While Ward waited for the appointed time, he began to work again on his sermon for Sunday, but his mind was elsewhere. He hoped that Dennis' business was not in some kind of trouble; or, that there had not developed a problem in Dennis' family. Neither seemed likely in view of what Ward knew about that family. In the vernacular, they were "the salt of the earth."

Of course, as head of one of the largest businesses in the nation, anything could have happened to cause a problem. Yet, Ward really doubted that, because he and Dennis had become very close during the thirty years of their friendship. Surely Ward would have been told of some ensuing problem. Dennis was not one of those few people who thought of the church only for "Matching; Hatching; and Dispatching"—as pastors often designated those who only came to the church for marriage, baptisms, and funerals.

Ward began to think back in time. It was just a few months ago that Dennis had headed the committee to celebrate Ward's thirty years of ordination and history in this congregation.

That celebration prompted Ward to think about those past thirty years. He remembered being anxious when he had first arrived as a novice pastor—well-trained, but being the one then responsible for the small congregation.

The worry was real, but unnecessary. God had been with Ward, and Ward had been a faithful pastor. He had been taught and believed that a

Christian is called to be faithful, not successful. If one were faithful, God would give the success.

That gift of success came over the decades. The congregation grew each year with Ward's faithful and hard work—especially so because many people had been drawn to this congregation because of the quality of his sermons. They were intelligent and meaningful because Ward followed the old premise that one hour of preparation was needed for each minute one preached. It was now a large group of dedicated Christians in an impressive building to house and support worship, education, fellowship, and mission of the congregation. Besides Ward, there were two other pastors and a full staff for administration, learning, and service to the large area of Indianapolis which surrounded the church buildings.

The other quality of Ward's pastoral ministry was that he spent a good portion of his work time simply visiting members in their home and in their places of work. He was a firm believer in that, understanding that—as the pastor—he needed to be in touch with the joys and needs of his people. Such dedication had slowly vanished in the style of many pastors, but Ward remembered what he had been taught.

He once read about a famous preacher who said, "I cannot preach under one thousand 'calls' a year." What that man meant was that a pastor/preacher needed to know about the lives of those people for whom he was responsible to God. It was also that—in "calling upon them"—he could then understand how God's Good News could apply to lives.

Too many people had been members of Christian congregations all their lives and never had a visit in their homes from any of their pastors. Ward was never that kind of pastor or leader.

That is why his congregation grew and prospered. He worked faithfully, and he worked many hours each week. Because of that—by the grace of God—the congregation grew. It was also the reason the members of that congregation also followed their pastor into "doing good works." Ward led and the people followed.

All of that fit in with Ward's personal understanding of the Christian faith and mission. He recalled a conversation he had with another pastor who commented about one of his own members. That pastor was somewhat disappointed with a woman who talked incessantly about her faith. However, she refused to get involved with helping in such outreach programs of his church as Meals on Wheels, visiting shut-ins, and aiding the congregation's senior citizens who simply needed physical help. That pastor's comment had been, "She is so heavenly that she is 'no earthly good.'" Ward thought the same could be said about many members of congregations. There were those who had simply forgotten who they were and why they had become members.

Actually, as Ward thought about it, the Bible is filled with such examples, as it talked about the "faithful remnant." That term could apply to any organization in any society. When an organization—or a congregation—was small, the members were compelled to be involved. Because of that, the organization grew and prospered. Finally, it reached a size and age when many of the members forgot why they belonged, so they became inactive and often left.

Those who remained—those who were dedicated to the principles of their membership—were the "faithful few." Once, again, those who remained became more dedicated as the process repeated itself. It was the duty of any organization to keep members in an active mode and thus prevent such a fall-out in numbers. Ward had developed a good process to accomplish that. It remained a challenging work, but it was easier to keep members than it was to obtain new ones.

His rambling thoughts were interrupted by the intercom: "Mr. Davies is here to see you, pastor." Ward immediately went to his office door and welcomed Dennis. "Come right in, Dennis. Good to see you again. When did you get home from your business in Europe?"

"Yesterday," was the response. "It's good to be at home. I would not have gone, but our business there has effects upon all of our factories throughout the U.S."

"Well, I'm glad to see that you made it home safely. And, I hope the trip was worth your time."

"It was very productive. I hope our meeting today will equal it," was Dennis' reply. That really piqued Ward's mind.

"Well, I must admit I have been intrigued. For our other meetings you always gave me information so I could do some preparing. You do have my attention. Please sit down and tell me what's happening."

There were a few cordialities spoken about family and church, but only a few. Then there was a short silence and Dennis began. "Pastor, there have been a lot of changes in our entire political system during the past decades. That is nothing new to you. You always seem knowledgeable about those things."

To state there had been a lot of changes in the political system was a very big understatement. What had transpired caused change at a basic level. While the growth of the political system in the nation had taken centuries, the change to what replaced it was quite rapid.

It had become a classic example proving that "Power corrupts; absolute power corrupts absolutely." There had been no one to blame but the politicians themselves. Just about everything they did was geared to getting re-elected. They became more powerful each term and also more wealthy. That growth in finances meant they had more money to spend to get re-elected again. It became a vicious circle. It isolated them more and more from the people they were supposed to represent. It even made them immune to the needs of people throughout the entire nation and world.

An early change forced by the voters was a system of term limits for every elected person, excluding the members of the U.S. Supreme Court. The situation had gotten so bad that one best-selling author even wrote a novel about term limits. The plot of the story was that certain members of Congress were being killed, along with the message that—unless long-term congress people resigned, they could be next on the list.

A Voters Organization went national in advocating term limits. Voters throughout the nation started a movement which informed every congressional candidate that if their vote was wanted, they each needed to promise they would introduce and vote for a six-year term limit for Congress. If that did not happen, they promised them defeat in any re-election. It took about a dozen years, but the voters finally got such a law passed. Congress now was entirely composed of six-year, one-term members.

Disgusted by political media ads, the voters also pushed thorough legislation forbidding any mention of one's opponent, prohibiting everything that might reveal what the candidate thought was wrong about the other person. Name-calling was prohibited. Also stopped was any hint of negativism. Candidates could only promote themselves and let the voters decide. It happened because the voters had determined there had to be a better way of electing and governing.

They slowly had begun to realize all political advertising was slanted. It was filled with many half-truths and complete falsehoods. Voters also secured a non-partisan group who checked all political ads and stopped any with lies, reporting such "lying" to the public.

Another change was a limit on the amount of money each candidate could spend during the campaign. Money had become the chief element in elections. It had reached a point where the cost of political campaigns for all of the candidates totaled into the billions of dollars. Most often the one who spent the most money became the winner. That had meant that the people did not really elect on the basis of issues. Even their choices on the ballot had been pre-determined—limited to people with an excess of money who simply announced their own "nomination" as a candidate. That meant the voters were limited in their choice right from the start.

Further, laws were passed limiting—and governing—lobbying. Corruption in that process meant that, technically, Congress did not make the laws. Unelected lobbyists were the real power in government. They gave the money that got "their people" elected, people who would propose and vote the way the contributing organization wanted.

A classic example of that corruption was one of the worst lobbyists in political history during the early years of the present century. One, particular lobbyist was earning over twenty million dollars a year in that position. Additional money—millions more—was given to him to "wine and dine" and fill the wallets of various, important members of Congress who agreed to vote the way the contributors wanted. It was even said at that time that Congress did not make the laws. The people for whom the lobbyists worked actually were the governing body of the nation.

That was quickly changed by an uprising of the voters. They simply rebelled against a process that spent hundreds of millions of dollars "buying congressmen." In fact, there was a saying that a certain politician was "the best congressman that money could buy." Voters also objected to the millions of dollars spent simply in the primaries, not to mention the sums spent each year on the political conventions. That had been lessened, but some of it yet remained.

Another change had been the elimination of the "Party System." The absence of that also removed a cause for a great deal of mismanagement. Too many issues were decided simply on party lines and not on the basis of worth. It was especially harmful when the outgoing administrative party simply stopped working as soon as the election results showed the other party had "won the white house." Even administrative supervision and oversight stopped during that transition time because "it's not our problem anymore. Let the new administration worry about it." It did not matter that the incoming administration had no power during the many weeks before it took office.

In addition, research had shown that most voters never even studied the issues involved, but simply voted for their party. The "party," not the "person," became the rallying point in the election process. The proof of that had been emphasized in the primary campaigns. Those candidates—in each party—ran down their opponents until one of them received the nomination. Then all of the former competitors were suddenly compelled to support the nominee as "the best person available."

With any "Party System" eliminated, those elected to Congress were no longer responsible to a particular "party" or point of view. Each congressman and senator could now listen to the debate concerning legislation and then vote as they saw fit, because they were responsible to the voters (and the nation) and not to some particular political party.

Naturally, Congress was yet composed of conservatives and liberals; and, of course, many moderates scattered between those two extremes. But there were no "party" affiliations. Each member's loyalty remained with self and with those he or she represented, and also with the welfare of the entire nation.

Even the entire method of nomination and elections was in the process of change. It had not been settled yet, but a great deal of agreement had been reached. It was hoped that the change would come to pass before the next presidential election

That final change was in the works. It had to do with the way voters nominate and elect the next president and vice president of the United States. With the six-year, one-time term limit, there never again would be an incumbent for the nation's highest office. It was already in place for Congress. Each person elected served only for six years. Then, they were no longer eligible for election to either house of Congress or president or vice president.

That process lessened the possibility of corruption in government. No elected official ever remained in office long enough to be tempted by anyone with money. It used to be true that only the rich, or those who had extreme financial backing, could ever hope at a chance at being elected to any national office. Now, there would no longer be any professional politician. People would be electing responsible, moral individuals who would lead professional staffs in their various roles.

"Well," Ward interjected, "I have had an interest in history—even political history—for a long time. I am very happy those changes came. I continue to be surprised they happened, but I'm glad they did."

"That's why I wanted to meet with you today," Dennis responded. "I would like to really test the new process for nominating and electing a president. It is going to be used for the first time this year. I have calculated the cost of time and money, and—for me—it is easily within reach."

Ward was excited by what Dennis said. "Wow! That's great! You'll have my vote."

"Thanks for the confidence, but that is not why I am here," Dennis continued. "I'm a little old and far too involved with my business to be thinking about that. While I believe no one is experienced enough to have that job, I do believe that your personality, skills, work ethic, and moral character are such that you do qualify to make a run for it."

"What do you mean?" Ward queried. "I have never thought of such a possibility for myself."

"Don't you understand it is now within reach for any citizen? That's basically what our Constitution declares."

"Anything is possible, but not everything is probable," was the cliché that popped into Ward's mind and out of his mouth.

"That's the beauty of the recent changes in the entire election process. With the prohibition of television and other expensive public persuasion tricks, what a candidate needs is mainly the ability to think. There are plenty of educated experts to give the president input on which to base a decision. I have seen you do that many times as a leader in this congregation.

"When you taught us about the Myers/Briggs Personality Type Indicators, you told us that you were an ESTJ type. That means that your major process is 'thinking.' That seems to tell me that you are an ideal candidate for president. For too many years we have had presidents who never thought about the present and future effects of their decisions."

"I don't know about all of that. Thank you for the compliment, but this whole thing is so immense and so unthinkable that I don't know what else to say at this point." Ward was obviously stunned at the thought.

Dennis grabbed at that. "Well, you have not said 'No!' and that is good. I just want you to think about the possibility. Talk with Lisa about it. Pray about it. Ask me questions about it. If you will say 'Yes' to that much, that you will at least consider it, that will be all that I ask.

"I do need to add something. I can make the attempt happen. I can't guarantee you will even make it through the entire process. But, in this new method of electing a president, you have as much of a chance as anyone else. The voters will decide.

"Remember that struggle to get things changed? It all started with the formation of a national voters' group. I think the anachronism for it was 'VACUUM.' If I remember it correctly, it stood for 'Voters against Congress' Useless, Unproductive Management,' or something like that."

"I remember that. It wasn't too many years ago. I also remember their reasoning for the term. It is a scientific fact that nature abhors a vacuum. Nature continually tries to fill it to recreate balance. That's what that voter group tried to do, and they did it." Ward was recalling much of his political study avocation.

"Well," Ward said after a little hesitation. His mind was working overtime and moving in a lot of directions. While he read a lot of articles about U.S. politics, he had never once thought about actually becoming a politician. Of course, he was familiar with the politics within congregations and the church at large. That had always been a topic for discussion at some church meetings and among pastors. But, this was so much bigger in scope. He continued, "I'll do what you suggested. I guess one of my concerns is that I am trained as a pastor. Also, I do enjoy that calling, especially as pastor of this congregation. It has been the only congregation I have served."

Dennis was ready for that. "I know that about you. I was here all those years. I saw you take us from a small, struggling group into a large, effective congregation.

"But your personality, training, experience, and character are the very things that would also aid you as our nation's leader. As far as the congregation goes, you have been here for thirty years and have never taken the proffered year-long sabbatical. That time is for you to do whatever you want. If you did not get elected, you could simply return here, enriched with a great experience. If you ultimately were elected president, there is no limit to how you could also serve God following your six-year term as President of the United States."

"You've answered one of my biggest questions before I even asked it. Thank you for that. So, I won't say 'No' without time for thought, prayer, and discussing it with Lisa. After that, I should be able to give you a 'No' or a 'Maybe.' When would you like to know?"

"We have plenty of time. We can meet again in two weeks. I will do some more detailed investigation and preliminary planning in anticipation of a positive response from you and Lisa, but don't let that influence your decision. I enjoy doing that kind of thing. It keeps my brain active, especially because it is different from the kind of stuff I have to do for my business.

"I also want to assure you that you will remain my pastor and my friend no matter what you determine to be your decision and God's will in this matter. The choice rests entirely with you, God, and Lisa. I just thank you for your time and your consideration."

Ward was emotionally exhausted when that brief meeting ended. What a way to begin the day! There were so many thoughts and emotions racing through his mind. He just sat back down at his desk, closed his eyes, and prayed.

Chapter 2:
"Communication Is Essential"

"What? What did you say?" Lisa was shocked and confused with Ward's first words to her. "He asked you to run for president? He did mean the President of the United States, didn't he?"

"That's why he wanted to see me today. It had nothing to do with his family or his business. I was relieved to know that. He just wanted to talk about running for president. At first, I thought he meant he was going to try for himself. But, no; he wanted me to do that. And, he asked me to talk with you about it. He also answered a few technical problems that popped into my mind. So, here I am and here you are."

Lisa jumped in as soon as he hesitated. "Are you certain that is what he meant? Are you sure that is what he said? Maybe you really do need hearing aids. You must not have heard him or you didn't listen to everything he said. Tell me, Ward, what exactly did Dennis say?"

Ward smiled a little at first. Lisa had often bugged him about his hearing: that either he needed aids or he had very selective hearing. It had been a "little joke" between them, but Ward was not so certain Lisa was always joking. He hesitated to remember Dennis' exact words. "Well, he said he wanted to test the new rules about the election of a president, including the presidential campaign. I thought he was talking about himself and told him I would vote for him. He immediately responded he was not thinking about himself, but he wanted me to do it. He said I should consider it, and he could make it possible for me to at least begin the process and see what happens."

Lisa shook her head and gave a sigh. "I'm having a problem digesting all of this. Wouldn't Dennis be more qualified to run than you? He's the owner and CEO of a large corporation. Isn't that the kind of leadership essential for a national president?"

Ward was thankful for these kinds of questions. Such an open discussion was necessary for both Lisa and him, no matter what the final decision or outcome. "Dennis is convinced that the primary requisite for the president of this nation is the ability to think. He believes the president is the one who should listen to all sides of an issue; then, think and pray about it; then, make a decision. I agree with that kind of process. I have done it most of my life. Remember, you are an INFP, but according to Myers/Briggs, I am an ESTJ, and 'thinking' is my major process. He also reminded me that I have the ability to deal with all three time periods in life: past, present, future. That, he said, is extremely important for a national leader."

"Oh, have you already decided what you are going to do?" Lisa asked with an upraised eyebrow and a smile.

"No. We are just discussing the possibility. We haven't even begun to think about more questions to ask Dennis—if we decide even to go that far with it.

"Remember, the President does not have as much power as people assume. The Constitution does outline a Separation of Powers. I have always been amused at former candidates for president who made all those promises 'if elected.' Congress makes the laws. The Supreme Court makes the interpretation. The Administration is to carry out those laws. That has not always happened in that way, but it needs to be done as the Constitution demands. If it isn't, we will revert to the turmoil we had during a few decades in our history.

"Of course, the president does have the power to suggest laws. And, he also has the power of the veto regarding laws that have been passed but not signed. But ultimate government is meant to rest in the people of this nation, carried out by their representatives in the Congress. Remember, we really are not a democracy. We are a republic and governed by representation. We are simply too large a nation to be governed by continuous vote of all the people."

"And Dennis believes that you are able to fit into all of this—enough to be president?"

Ward shrugged his shoulders, smiled, and said, "That's his opinion, and apparently he is willing to bet some of his time on it. Or, I could decline, telling him I believe the best form of government is a monarchy—if I can be king."

"That's an old joke, even if you don't mean it." Lisa was smiling, but she had heard Ward say that many times in the past.

"Now, I don't know what my odds would be, but Dennis is hoping that at least we will agree to try. That is why we need to discuss it. And that is why we need to ask a lot of questions before we say 'Yes' or 'No.'"

Lisa's mind began with these questions, "Don't you need to be a lawyer? What about your work as a pastor? What about my work as a nurse? What about…"

Ward stopped her: "One thing at a time! No, the president does not need to be a lawyer. Maybe it would be better if the president were not a lawyer. Lawyers in government have a habit of working for laws which would benefit them if they don't get re-elected and defeating laws which would harm them in private practice. Natural Citizenship and minimum age are the only restrictions. Actually we had at least two presidents who were generals, not lawyers: Grant and Eisenhower."

"At least you fulfill those two requirements, even if you don't have any other qualifications," was Lisa's injection.

Ward smiled and went on. "As to being pastor here, Dennis explained that I have a year's sabbatical available, and it could be used for me to make a 'run' as far as it takes me. Now, it is possible I might be 'out of the running' when the first cut is made."

"It is also very 'probable'," Lisa sort of joked again, stressing a sense of reality. "But, now I forget what else I wanted to ask and question. It does seem that Dennis has given all of this a great deal of thought. But, this entire thing is quite overwhelming to me."

"I know. I feel the same. That is because great minds think alike," Ward joked about it. "But we need to think about it and come up with a definite decision within the next two weeks. While we do that, Dennis is going to investigate details. He will meet with us then to hear what we have to say and answer any further questions we have. I think we owe him at least that, even if our decision is 'Thanks, but no thanks.'"

After a few moments of silence, Lisa gave Ward a hug and spoke softly, "Alright, I can do that much. That gives me two weeks to dream and pretend I am the First Lady, living in the White House."

Ward broke the hug and gave Lisa a tender kiss. "No matter what happens, you will always be my 'first lady.' Enjoy the dream, but don't start planning how to redecorate the White House yet. It's always pleasant to pretend.

"We'll let it rest for a couple of days. We can each write down questions and ideas before we talk about it again." Lisa nodded in agreement as Ward left on his way back to the church.

Chapter 3:
"Anticipation Is Not All That Bad"

The two weeks passed by rather pleasantly for Lisa, even though she was skeptical about the reality what was happening. Even so, it was rather nice to think about the prospect, no matter how remote the possibility. At least there was the fun of imagining what it would be like. Anticipation always was like that—bringing a joy that may or may not come to fruition. If she and Ward both said "Yes," at least there would be the excitement of entering the process.

Just for fun, she began to think about living in the White House: how that might be with all of the staff and excitement. She also began to imagine herself as First Lady—how she might act; how she would relate to all those important people. Those two weeks went by quickly, helped by her usual duties as wife, mother of adult children, and nurse in the local hospital. It was all like a dream—a game in which the impossible happened to both of them, even though she was actually a pessimist by nature.

Those same days were not as pleasant for Ward. Even though he was an optimist by nature, he recognized this would probably be the third most important decision of his life: the first being his response to God; the second being his marriage to Lisa.

Without sacrificing too much time from his pastoral duties—by the grace of God (he thought)—at least there had been a slack in the demand for his time during those two weeks, particularly the absence of any real emergencies that needed his immediate attention. That did give him more time for his prayers. Now, there were not only prayers for his church family, world peace, the environment, the sick and dying, but also for God's help and direction for Lisa and him in the discussion and final decision regarding this new proposal.

He, too, had spent some time thinking about what he might be able to accomplish for people if he was the president. He knew that one of his responsibilities as a Christian—as well as a world citizen—was to do what he could to make things better in both creation and population. Both of those tasks were a part of the mission of his congregation. Both had been a part of his own life for some time.

A smile came to his face. He recalled the old joke he had told Lisa when they first discussed this—what he had often jokingly told people: "I believe a monarchy is the best form of government—if I could be king." Being president was a long way from being king, but it had more opportunities for doing good things for the nation than merely being a pastor.

Chapter 4:
"Decisions Cannot Be Avoided"

Eventually, those fourteen days passed. Ward and Lisa had spent time discussing all the pros and cons and had come up with questions for Dennis. They were presently inclined—depending on the answers—to agree to start the process and see what happened. Maybe God really did want them to try it.

Dennis came to their home early one evening and they sat down at the dining room table, Dennis with his briefcase and Ward and Lisa with their own sheets of paper. There were just a few preliminary greetings and then Dennis got right to the point. "Well, I have checked all the details, and I am convinced you have a chance—even though it is slight and the odds are extreme. With the new process in place, all that we need to start are one million names on the nomination papers."

Ward and Lisa quickly looked at each other and together said, "That ends that." Ward continued alone, "There is no way for that to happen. I don't even know more than a few thousand people."

"No," Dennis continued, "that isn't a problem. I will take care of it. First of all, there are thousands of people here in Indianapolis who would like to see a 'hometown boy' enter the race. In addition, I have factories all over the country, so it will not be difficult to obtain those signatures. With my recommendation, those nomination papers will be done quite rapidly. The only purpose of requiring a million signatures is to limit the number of people available on the first, local ballot.

"People know me. They trust me. I have always treated people fairly. Also, I have believed a person's name is of value. Success in this nomination stage will prove me right. Trust me. All that the two of you have to do is to sign the paper yourself. We begin with both your names so we only have 999,998 to go."

"Wow!" Lisa gave a smiling response. "We are almost there."

"I know you are joking," Dennis said with a smile, "but you need to trust me on this. With the connections I have in my business, I am not the least bit worried. I have already made inquiries and gotten very positive support. There are a lot of people in this nation who are happy with the political changes already in place and are eager to test them even further in the election of a president and vice-president."

Ward scratched his head and searched for the right words. "I understand, Dennis, but we do have a few questions before we make such a monumental decision." He was searching for a way to thank Dennis for his work so far; yet, he wanted more information before they said 'Yes.'

What happened next was a very frank discussion about the steps following the filing of the nomination papers. It was difficult for Ward and Lisa to comprehend that Dennis could arrange for one million plus people to sign and support nomination for U.S. President of someone they had never met or known, but they trusted him because he had always been a man of his word.

They talked and discussed the elimination process—how the many nominees would eventually dwindle down to ten persons through various forms of selection by those in the general population who were interested enough to read resumes and vote. Dennis did explain that Ward needed to write up his own resume, limited to five hundred words. The government would print that and a submitted picture of Ward in a booklet along with those from other nominees from Ward's region. That booklet—the only "political information" allowed at the opening stage—would be mailed to every household in his region.

There were ten regions in the nation, but residents would vote first only for those in their own region. Within four weeks, the vote in each region would be held. If there were more than ten nominees, each voter would vote for five names. That gave each person a first, second, third, fourth, and fifth choice—a voting procedure that was determined to be much fairer to all concerned. The top ten names in each region would then have been selected, and another vote would be held in one month.

In a month the second vote would be taken, with each voter choosing three names, ranking their choices as first, second, third. First place was worth three points; second place was worth two points; and third place was worth one point. The person with the highest number of points would "win" the region and become a finalist—ten nominees in the entire nation.

Dennis continued to explain the reasoning behind this process. "This same pattern is also used when the final vote for president is taken. Giving people more than one choice assures that the winners are really the correct choice of the majority of voters. It will also be true in the selection of the vice president. That person will have received the second most points for president in the final vote rather than being picked by the presidential nominee and then automatically elected at a national party convention.

"So, after all ten regions—which have been determined on the basis of population – have each selected their one candidate, those ten names will be placed on a national ballot. At that time, each nominee is permitted to establish a website and another booklet would be printed and mailed by the government to all voters in the nation. That booklet will contain the original resume, along with the website address of each of the ten finalists.

"Again, voters will vote for first, second, and third place. Those votes each will be graded with points, so that it is possible that a second place could end up with more points than first place votes. The person with the most points is elected president and the person with the second most points is elected vice president. In this way, it is the people who really decide the outcome for both offices."

"That seems rather complicated," was Lisa's contribution to the discussion.

Ward quickly answered, "But it really is a more accurate way of doing it. Just think. When given a second choice, there can easily be many more people who prefer number two than who prefer number one. I remember learning that many years ago. With the old method, the 'winners' seldom—if ever— were the 'favorites.'"

Dennis then continued. "The votes are graded so the voters' number one choice would get three points for each vote, and number two gets two points, and the third choice gets one point—similar to the process used in the regional contests. That process makes number one more valuable, but it also guarantees a huge majority for number two—who did not vote for number one—yet have a say in the election. With ten names on the ballot, it might even be possible for that third choice to become president.

"Along with that," Dennis continued, "we have eliminated the political advertising which was dishonest as well as costly. That was money that can be put to better use, like food for the hungry and housing for the homeless. It is amazing what a political campaign had cost before those changes were made. Perhaps 'amazing' is not the correct word. Actually, it was a sinful waste.

"No longer would communications organizations bank tens of millions of dollars from political advertising. Ended, also, are the huge political rallies, attended only by 'elected' party supporters—all of whom were not even required—after the first ballot—to vote for the person designated.

"Now we have taken away the privilege from the politicians and given all that power to the people, where it belongs. The former income—lost by the media—now has to be earned in other ways or in decreased operational expenses."

Ward and Lisa had followed a lot of that history. They had talked about it somewhat in the previous two weeks. It was because they thought the changes were hopeful that they had arrived at this important opportunity in their lives—why they even agreed to discuss the possibility with Dennis.

Dennis continued. "The time is right to see what happens when non-politicians test the new process. It is now possible for just about anyone to start a campaign, if they can get one million signatures. I have already told you I will take care of that. So, do you have further questions?"

Ward and Lisa looked at each other. Ward decided to ask first. "What about expenses in all of this? It has to cost something for the campaign."

"The government takes care of the initial publication and mailing costs and the voting expenses. If you make it to the final ten candidates, there will be some travel expense, but it will be minor, and I will take care of it. It will be much less than what is allowed. I have been told there will be only one debate. It will be in New York, and it will be televised on all networks.

"In order to make up for the other political advertising, the government is allowing commercial advertising during the debate. The media should do quite well because the size of the TV audience is expected to be immense. That means very expensive commercial ads."

"But, as I understand it, there will not be any political ads. Correct?" Ward interjected.

"Correct!" was Dennis' response. "In fact, it is so well supervised that I cannot even buy a TV ad for that broadcast for my company because my name is on your nomination paper. Every item in the new election process is being watched very carefully. No longer will money influence elections as it did before."

"What a huge change that is!" Lisa was amazed at the details. "It used to be that political ads could even lie about an opponent and no one did anything about it. There was no one in government who was responsible for it."

Lisa had known about many of the changes that had been voted, but she had not thought about all of the specific details. "I hate to say it, but all of this is really a drastic—but wonderful—difference. It has brought out more voters than ever before. I guess they now believe that voting will finally accomplish some good." Lisa smiled at Ward and continued, "I think it would be an exciting experience to have a 'go' at it. How do you feel about it?"

Nodding approval, Ward smiled at her and asked, "Are you saying 'Yes!' to all of this? Do you agree to have a 'go' at it?"

"Why not? At least you would have your 'fifteen minutes of fame.' It might even be fun."

Ward turned back to Dennis and said, "Okay, Dennis. We will make the attempt. You have made a good case for at least trying."

Dennis was pleased with the decision. "Thank you. Just remember there is no promise you will even survive the first vote, much less finally reach the White House. The odds are tremendously against it, but, with each victory the odds get better. We just need to take one step at a time and see what happens.

"In case you don't remember, if you would become president or vice president, both your health insurance and your pension would be in the social security system. The voters forced that change just two years ago."

Ward nodded. "I remember that happening. I never thought it would affect me as a pastor, except as a greater guarantee for the continuance of social security. I know I favored such a change because it simply was not fair that those elected to office had better insurance and retirement than we voters."

Dennis was pleased with Ward's understanding. "Now, I do hope the change will directly affect you as a winner in this election."

"It was a great advance for our nation," Ward responded with a smile, "but, the odds are I won't even make it that far in the election. So, when I retire, I will have my church health and retirement funds along with my social security and Medicare."

Ward was the first to rise. "We just need to thank you now for making that first step happen. I guess I am starting to get both excited and nervous. I haven't felt this way since I got married and when our children were born." He looked at both Dennis and Lisa as he said that. Lisa blew him a kiss.

Dennis shook Ward's hand and gave Lisa a hug. As he left the room he reminded them, "Your next task is to prepare your five-hundred word resume and attach a three-by-three photo. We'll meet next week at this same time to critique it. And, thanks again for taking me up on this proposal. It means a great deal to me." He started to leave, but then stopped. "Oh, I almost forgot. We need think about a website, just in case you become one of the finalists. I'll get started on that right away. It should contain your resume and anything else you might think about. It is another, permissible way of communicating with voters."

When Dennis left, Ward and Lisa looked at each other. Then, without a word, they hugged each other, shared an "I love you," and embraced in a long kiss. Both wondered what the future would bring them.

It was Ward who broke the kiss. "I just remembered. The only pictures I have of myself are those in which I am wearing a clerical collar. I don't think that would be appropriate for this. I need to have a different picture taken."

Ward always wore his clerical collar while working as a pastor. Some of his colleagues accused him of even having clerical pajamas; a few asked to see his clerical swimming suit. But, he told them he wore the clerical shirt to remind others that he was a pastor and—more importantly—to remind himself he was a pastor and should "act like it." So, the next day he dressed in a suit, shirt, and tie while having a picture taken.

BOOK THREE

Chapter 1:
"Life Is Filled With New Beginnings"

"Here is the first draft of my resume," Ward spoke as he handed Lisa the paper. "I got up early to work on it. Actually, my mind was working on it ever since Dennis left last night. I don't know how much I even slept."

"Oh, I think you did alright in that department. I was tossing a lot and I don't remember waking you. Just the thought of being on the first ballot is exciting. Whatever happens after that would just be 'frosting on the cake.'"

"Well, in between your naps on the couch today, read this over and write down your thoughts, ideas, suggestions, what you don't like, and anything that pops into that beautiful head of yours. We only have six days before we need to discuss it with Dennis."

They had agreed upon that style of discussing things related to the campaign. Both of them were to write down their own ideas and give a copy to the other for written critiques. After that they would sit down and discuss them and make a decision. Ward had used that kind of process throughout his ministry, and he liked it so much that he was not about to change it. He knew this was a better way to begin any discussion and decision.

Ward has used that process for many years and learned its value. It was the best way to stimulate original thoughts from each person involved before they would be prejudiced by someone else's suggestions. That way all discussion and decisions would be completely considered before formulating final plans.

An additional benefit of such a process was that much of the "thinking" was done by one's brain during the time between an original thought and a final decision. Whenever he had been stumped in his work—whether it was preparing sermons, working on lectures, preparing for meetings, and all other issues—Ward would simply stop and do some work that was different. It was amazing how much clearer the original problems became after the human mind worked on them while a person did something else, even while sleeping.

"How about giving me an advance payment for my work on this?" Before she could say anything else, Ward drew her close and gave her a very passionate kiss. She dropped that sheet of paper and threw her arms around him. "That will keep me awake for a while. I'll collect the final payment when I'm finished with my work for you."

Ward smiled, but simply answered, "I do have some office work to finish. I'll be home for lunch." Then he left for the church.

Lisa smiled as she watched him leave. Then she picked up the resume she had dropped. It didn't seem like much to summarize the fifty-one years of Ward's life. Then she remembered that Ward did have a way with words—the ability to say a lot in a few words. Someone had once commented that he "wrote tight," meaning that editors had a difficult time shortening what he wrote simply by removing unnecessary words. He seldom wrote such unnecessary words. In fact, he never even read a lot of things sent to him when they were too lengthy. His excuse was that "if the author did not spend the time and effort to eliminate redundancy in his writing, why should I bother doing that work for him?" Another of his favorite sayings was "I could never speak long enough to emphasize the importance of brevity."

Lisa walked over to the couch and made herself comfortable, a pillow here and a pillow there, and then she stretched out. As she started to read the resume, an entire series of events in her history with Ward passed through her mind. Every notation reminded her of their life together. Even the notation about high school made her think back to that first day they met at their school lockers. Then there was the way he asked her for their first date. But, before she had read a little more than half of the resume, she fell asleep, just as Ward had hinted she would do.

It was about an hour later, when she turned over in her sleep, that she fell to the floor. Now she was awake again. She decided that she needed to sit up to study the resume—rather than doing it while horizontal—so that she could finish her critique before she needed to prepare lunch. She did not want to tell Ward about falling asleep because he would tease her about it.

During lunch, Ward simply asked her if she had finished, and she was able to tell him she had. Then Ward reminded her that she should think about other things until they talked about the resume in the evening.

That night, Lisa and Ward went over the resume, making just a few changes. Then they met again with Dennis and the three of them critiqued it together. After a minor change suggested by Dennis, Ward printed up the finished product and gave it and his new picture to Dennis to forward to the government agency in charge of the election.

RESUME: 2052 AD
Ward Roy Adamson

BORN: June 18, 2001
EDUCATION:
6/2/2019 – Milwaukee North High School

6/5/2023 – BA: Penn State University; Double Major of English & History; with special study in U.S. Political History

5/30/2027 – MST: Yale Divinity School

5/28/2047 – PHD: Yale University

EXPERIENCE: 6/1/2027 to the present: Lead Pastor & CEO of Grace Lutheran Church (3500 members), Indianapolis, IN.

Indiana State Board of Education Member

Indianapolis City Development Chairperson

National Lutheran Church Executive Board member

PERSONAL: Married 34 years; 2 children; 3 grandchildren

BASIC PHILOSOPHY: As an ESTJ personality (Myers/Briggs), my major process is "Thinking"—listening to all sides of an issue and then able to think it through to its final consequence. At that point, I have the ability to be very decisive in my decision. I believe that the most important element is to surround oneself with a variety of—even differing—opinions. That means I want to surround myself with the very best people.

I live my life and my work guided by certain "truisms." Encased in them are all kinds of truths about who we should be and how we should act—both as individuals, and also as a nation.

"The END never justifies the MEANS used to obtain it."

"Honesty is the best policy."

"The family is the basic building block of society."

"Pray as though everything depends upon God—Work as though everything depends upon you."

"Government is 'of the people, for the people, and by the people.'"

"Say what you mean and mean what you say."

"We have met the enemy and he is us."

"Love is an active verb rather than a noun."

"It all depends upon whose ox is being gored."

"When you don't understand something, follow the money trail."

"A penny saved is a penny earned."

"Whoever does not remember the past is condemned to repeat it."

Chapter 2:
"Now It Gets Serious"

The government printed the booklets containing the resumes of all those who had submitted nomination papers containing the necessary signatures. That meant that all the voters in each of the ten regions received a booklet of the resumes of those nominees in their own region. In Ward's region there were nineteen nominees, so every resident or family in that region received a booklet with nineteen resumes. If there were only ten or less nominees in a region, the first vote was not needed to get the number down to ten.

At that point in the process, that was the only information allowed. No one was permitted to take out ads or endorsements of any kind. Neither were there any "letters to the editor" allowed. Those kinds of suggestions to vote for a particular nominee had become a serious problem in former years. People were entitled to their opinions and could talk privately about their own choice, but not in any media form where false information could not be challenged.

That proposal had caused a great deal of controversy—centered on the issue of "free speech." There had also been the argument that the national government could not dictate to the states such prohibitions. The arguments went all the way to the U.S. Supreme Court, where the ruling was finally made: the states make the rules for their own state, county and city elections, but Congress makes the rules for national elections.

The use of the internet for political campaigning was also prohibited at this stage. That applied to all the candidates and also to the general public. Recent developments had made it possible to check the internet to such a degree that anyone trying to bypass that law faced prosecution. That possibility came about because government needed to end the dangerous internet bullying started decades ago. It took a few suicides and more intelligent technology to accomplish, but now such control was possible. The one exception to that rule was that the winner in each region was able to establish his or her own website after being elected to the national ballot. But, that site could not even mention the other candidates or contain any negative ideas about them and their views.

The voting would be held on a date two weeks following the receipt of the booklets. Each voter was to vote for five candidates. To vote for less (or more) than five persons would invalidate the ballot. In this first vote, the top ten persons would continue in the process, and another vote would be taken in two weeks.

In that second vote in each region, the ballot required voting for three persons out of the ten remaining, also ranking them as to "first, second, and third choice"—with three, two, and one points for each choice. The person with the highest number of points would then become the winner of that region. That person, and one from each of the other nine regions, would become the finalists. The next president and vice president would come from that list after the next voting. It was at that point that each of the ten candidates was allowed to establish a website.

Chapter 3:
"At the Starting Line"

The needed signatures for the nomination papers had been collected in a reasonably short time, considering the enormity of the task. It was as Dennis had promised. His many employees and contacts in their region wasted no time in indicating with signatures that they were ready for a better way of electing the next president and vice president. People were also pleased with the absence of the obnoxious politics of the previous system. Voters also appreciated the financial savings and the freedom from the lack of political ads and unsolicited telephone calls. The biggest problem in all of that kind of campaigning was the half-truths and blatant lies spread by all of the candidates. They had done that for decades because they knew most voters did not remember what had happened even a few years ago.

Step by step the campaign moved forward. A very surprised—and pleased—Ward and Lisa read the report as Ward's name remained on the second ballot: the final vote for the region. One of those persons would become the regional nominee as the campaign moved into the national arena for the final step.

"I never would have believed I would get even this far," was all that Ward could say, shaking his head in his amazement. "I thought my 'ministerial' background would have eliminated me right away. It is humbling and exalting at the same time."

"Well, don't start packing yet." Lisa was eager to put realism back into the conversation. "The odds have not improved that much for you. The next vote is the important one. Only one of those ten names will be on the final ballot."

"I knew I could count on you to bring me back to reality. I do need that. Humility is not my greatest virtue." Ward smiled after he spoke and gave Lisa a peck on her cheek. "There was a time I thought about writing a book titled

Perfect Humility, and How I Achieved It. The opening page would have a group picture of me. One of the chapters would be, "How to Pat Yourself on Your Back without Breaking Your Arm.'" Lisa laughed and gave him a kiss.

There was nothing to do for the campaign during the next two weeks. Ward kept busy in his pastoral duties. That kept his mind off politics fairly well, but humorous—and supportive—comments from those around him did produce a slight change in his normal life and work.

Instead of starting out with a sabbatical year, he had decided that, with this new system of no campaigning, he would only use some of his vacation time for any campaign issues. If he lasted longer in the process, he could always simply rely on sabbatical time.

After voting for the second time in the regional contest, Ward and Lisa took the rest of the day off. They had invited a few friends over for dinner that night, mainly for the company. They would periodically receive updates on the results of the vote, but both of them were low key about Ward's chances.

Dennis and his wife arrived early to see if they could help with the dinner. There were a few items left in the preparation for the dinner, but that did not take long. The four of them finally relaxed and began to talk only about their families—how everyone was doing and any new family updates. Ward did ask Dennis how his business was going, especially because Dennis had spent a part of his time on campaign items.

In a short time the others began to arrive. Snacks and cocktails were served and friendly conversation filled the time until dinner was served. Lisa led the prayer before dinner, intentionally avoiding any mention of the voting, and all began to enjoy what she had prepared.

After dinner, several of the women offered to help, and Lisa accepted. The men returned to the living room and Ward started the conversation, beginning with sports. That was intentional, because he hoped to avoid anything political. The others sensed what he was doing and they all followed suit, even after the women had finished and joined them. Of course, then, the conversation changed to things like family, business, and health.

It was later in the evening when the election results came. Dennis had made arrangements for the regional results to be phoned to him. When his telephone rang, he excused himself and went into the other room. After a few moments he returned with the phone in his hand and the speaker turned on. "Will you repeat that now," he said.

A voice came over the speaker, "Ward Adamson took first place and is now one of the national ten finalists!"

The living room broke into shouts and applause. Ward was stunned and bowed his head, either in a prayer of "Thank you" or one of "Help!" as Lisa looked at him and grabbed his hand. Both were really stunned, wondering about what they heard and what would happen next.

People began to get up and walk over to Ward and Lisa, congratulating and hugging them. It was simply astounding to all of them that their pastor was one of the ten finalists for the office of President of the United States.

After all but Dennis and his wife had left, the four of them sat down and talked about the future. The next item on the agenda was the development of a website. Dennis had already been thinking about it because he always planned ahead for various possibilities. "I have an employee who works with our business website. Tomorrow, I'll have him plan a couple of site styles for you. When he is done, I'll give you a call and we will review them. Meanwhile, why don't the two of you write down some suggestions regarding what you want to have on the site and how you want to use it?"

Ward had little to say. He really was shocked at how the odds had changed in the last month. "Thank you, Dennis. I simply can't think at this point, but Lisa and I will think about all of this. Just call me when you want us to meet again."

Dennis and his wife left. Ward and Lisa hugged both of them, again thanking them for their support and work. When the door closed, Ward and Lisa silently looked at each other, and then they embraced. It was time to talk a little and then go to bed. The evening had drained a lot of energy from both of them. The possibilities of the future were mind-boggling, and they both had tears in their eyes. Following just a few, loving words to each other, they went to bed.

Chapter 4:
"In the National Spotlight"

Each of the ten finalists was allowed a website, governed by certain rules. The chief prohibition was that sites were not to mention or be negative about any other candidate. Under the two-party system, candidates in each party were accustomed to accusing other primary candidates in their own party of many faults. But, after one was finally nominated, all in each party became extremely supportive of the nominee, forgetting every bad thing they had ever spoken about him or her during the primary.

The new system was planned to be positive and honest in every respect. This meant that even the websites were checked by members of the media for accuracy. It has always been that those in public life were fair game when it came to the truth. That was especially true with the website for each of the finalists.

In a month, another booklet would be sent out to the nation by the government, using only the previous resumes of the ten finalists plus a website address for each. The websites were meant to give additional information about each candidate: down-to-earth description and personal history, family picture, management style, etc.

One of Ward's ideas was to include a "Suggestion Box" so anyone could e-mail him ideas about how to improve life in the United States. A note was added, promising that such an e-mail "suggestion box" would become a permanent part of one of his ways of communication with people, if he were elected president.

It took only a few days before they all met again—Ward, Lisa, Dennis, and John, the website person for Dennis' company. There were many items from which to select. It took about two hours to come to a final decision, but then it was done. Within a few days the website was on the internet.

It took only one day after the voters received the second booklet that Ward's site had hundreds of responses. Lisa volunteered to help sort them out and write down a few important ones for Ward. He thought it would be polite to try and briefly respond to as many as possible. Within a week, he simply added to his website an appreciation for all of the suggestions and questions, but that he would no longer have the time to respond to so many because he did not have the staff to do that. He would keep all suggestions and ideas for discussion if he were elected.

Life really changed now for Ward and Lisa. There were many letters, both personal and political. They were now known—at least in name—throughout the nation and beyond. Most of the world was watching the new way of electing a national president. It had been true for several generations that people around the world were aware of what happened in the politics of the United States. The reverse of that was not very common among U.S. citizens.

High on the agenda for them was the debate for the ten finalists. There would be only one because that was in agreement with the philosophy of the new process. The election was to be based on the information already provided, and not on debating skills or arguments. That debate was in two weeks and would be held in New York City at Madison Square Garden. The television broadcast of that single debate would give the entire nation the only physical exposure possible with this new electoral way. Spending restrictions had eliminated the expensive campaigning tours and various media advertising. Voters were pleased with that because it meant that no candidate would become obligated to "repay" their financial supporters with government jobs, passage of laws favoring "supporting" businesses, etc.

The reasoning behind all of this was to eliminate the immense financial contributions to a candidate. Such money was given in the expectation that the contributor's winning candidate would favorably respond to the contributor's wants. With no such contributions allowed, the winners could concentrate on what was good for the nation, rather than what was wanted by the contributors. The same result came about with the outlawing of lobbying. People were now being elected to make decisions about the nation without the influence of special interest groups and individuals. One survey had shown that members of Congress had voted for up to eighty percent for laws favoring their own contributors. In addition, term limits assisted in keeping politicians from becoming too powerful, and then often corrupt.

Next in line for Ward was to prepare for the national debate. Ward, Lisa, and Dennis exchanged ideas about getting certain people to join them in the preparation—someone knowledgeable in foreign affairs, domestic programs, social services, etc. There was no end to the possibilities.

Ward finally held up his hand and interrupted the conversation: "Wait a minute! There is no way that I could accumulate enough knowledge in all those areas. For the debate, I want to be just who I am. I have always kept up with the news. I do a lot of reading. I don't want this to turn into a contest of who has the broadest knowledge of the entire world. If elected, I would surround myself with experts in all those fields—even those with opposing views. That is how I have always operated, and I will not change that."

Dennis thought for a few moments and then agreed. "You are right. You got this far just by being yourself."

The decision was made to continue in that manner. Ward's emphasis would remain that his leadership style was to surround himself with the best and most knowledgeable people to keep him informed about all sides of every issue. That would be the basis for all his decisions. So far, it seemed that such a person was what the voting public wanted, and Ward could not be other than who he was.

Therefore, the next two weeks were spent by Ward being busy with what he had done for so many years—working as a pastor. That also kept his mind off the excitement of what was happening to him. From time to time he would look at his website in order to read comments and suggestions that had been received. But, very soon there were so many that Lisa and a few of her friends also assisted, condensing and arranging ideas into groups so Ward would not have to go through all of the details more than once.

Ward also made a note that this website process should be continued in the new administration, no matter which person was elected. It was a way to break through the isolation that happened in the presidential office. Too many presidents in history simply were not aware of the thoughts and cares and needs of the general public. Ward was certain that such a process would really help make the United States a government of, for, and by the people.

Chapter 5:
"The Really Big Apple"

W ard and Lisa packed for the trip to New York. Dennis would also be there because he had been able to get an extra ticket to be in the audience for the debate. He would also be staying in the same hotel he had reserved for Ward and Lisa. Again, the cost was handled by Dennis—once more, all within the financial limits prescribed for this better way of electing a president and vice president.

When the evening of the debate arrived and all were ready for it to begin, Ward looked out over the crowd from the same podium he had stood behind earlier in the day. By the luck of the draw, Ward was to be the last of the ten candidates to give a brief opening statement about themselves and whatever else they chose to say. That was to his liking. It would be helpful for him to hear what the others had to say in order to frame his own remarks. He would go with his own strengths, but he also had the ability to think clearly about what the others had to say and relate it to his own views.

Ward had listened carefully as each of the other nine gave their three-minute introductions. Now it was his turn. "My name is Ward Adamson and I am surprised, humbled, and happy to be here among this group of nominees; chosen by the voters of our respective districts. I entered this challenging endeavor because this new process made it possible. I believe it is a much better way of electing anyone to our highest office. I also entered my name because someone suggested to me that I would make a good president.

"For years I have listened to the professional politicians as they made their promises in order to be elected, and voters tended to believe them—in spite of the fact that they were dreams, and often they were lies. Many of those promises were never kept. I will make no such promises because the president of this nation does not have the power to assure that most of those promises become reality. Remember, it is Congress that makes the laws. It is the

Supreme Court that interprets those laws. It is the Administration which puts those laws into practice. There has always been that separation of powers. It makes this Republic work. It fails whenever the Administration, the Congress, or the Supreme Court usurp from others any power not given to itself. The Constitution must be upheld and followed or it must be changed by the American voters.

"The one promise I am able to assure you is this: If I am voted by you to be the next president of these United States of America, I promise you every decision on every issue will be made with thorough, honest, and debated discussion. The best asset I can bring to this office is that 'thinking' is the main process of my personality. Whatever decisions I would need to make will always invite input—even from those opposed to the proposition. I will not operate within an insulated environment. For me, the will of the people is the guide for our unique form of democracy. To that end, I seek and will appreciate your vote. Thank you for your participation in this privilege."

The first of the three moderators spoke right after Ward—as the last nominee to introduce himself—had finished. "Thank you to all of you for your introductions. We now go to the questions, which have been prepared by our panel. Each of you will have one minute to answer. The light by your microphone will go on when the time starts and begin blinking with ten seconds remaining. Your mike will then be turned off when the sixty seconds have passed. We begin with Mrs. Nanfield. Are you basically conservative or liberal in your views?"

Ward was third in line with the same question. He said what he had told people for years. "I am either a Liberal Conservative or a Conservative Liberal. If you tell me the issue, I will tell you what I am on that particular issue." Ward got a laugh from the audience, but Ward wondered how well that description of himself had been received. There really was no way to determine that. No applause of agreement was allowed at the debate. The vote—finally— would tell the story.

One by one the remaining seven nominees answered the question. It went quickly. Only one person went too long and was in the middle of a sentence when his microphone was silenced. There had been a variety of differences in the answers. Mostly, they were fairly evenly divided in their answers, with one person dramatically insisting he was always a moderate.

Basically, the debate went quite smoothly. During the rest of the questions, different opinions were expressed, but it seemed that Ward's opening statement about not making promises had hit home with the other nine nominees. A lot of the statements were somewhat vague—some even seemed to miss the point of the issue. Ward remembered what he had been taught: that the most important item in conversations and discussions was the ability to listen to what is stated and even think about what is said "between the lines." He also remembered the old "clinker" that God created us with two ears and only one mouth. Ward's responses often contained his position of listening to the most knowledgeable people on both sides of the issue before making a decision one way or the other.

At the end, the three moderators each thanked the ten nominees for their time and their willingness to be a part of the entire process. Then the audience gave a standing ovation to all of them. It seemed the voters were really excited with and in favor of this better way of electing a new administration. Now they could focus on individuals and issues rather than on political parties. In addition, these final ten persons had been nominated and voted for by the people. No longer were they basically voting for people who had enough money to simply announce their candidacy and "nominate" themselves at a press conference.

It was also going to be true that the voters would have to vote for individuals. The ballots would no longer have a simple "Party Vote" that could be checked at the polls. People would now have to think and decide for themselves and then check off their choices on the ballot. No longer would voters be swayed by the party that spent the most money on political ads. Gone were the "attack" ads. The voters had decided and had given the message: "Don't tell me what and whom you are against. Tell me what you are for!"

After the debate, Ward and the others remained on the stage and greeted each other. It remained very cordial, with no hint of any animosity. It was a gathering of like-minded people who were more interested in serving their nation, than in how it might benefit them and their friends.

The moderators came up on stage. From time to time they expressed similar feelings about the candidates and the evening. The new process had come a long way. The next step was up to the voters, and a record turn-out was predicted. The attitude of the voters had changed dramatically, so much so, that polls indicated that at least eighty percent of eligible voters now would cast their ballots.

Chapter 6:
"What's Fair Is Fair for All"

The Final Vote would happen in two weeks: on the first Tuesday in November. All ten names would be on the ballot, but that was the not the only change this time. Voters were required to choose three of the nominees for president. They were also to mark those three as to their first choice, and their second choice, and their third choice. Such a method gave the voters an additional "say" in the election of the president.

While it had always been stated—after the election—that the president had been chosen by the majority of the "people," the truth was that probably never happened. Elections were won on the basis of the majority of the voters who voted, not the majority of the people able to vote.

Added to that was the fact that in the old system, the voters did not really "nominate" any candidates. They were able to choose only between those who had nominated themselves.

However, the big difference was the ability and requirement of each voter to make a second and third choice from among the ten finalists. This eliminated the usual results produced by having to choose between more than two candidates on the ballot. That had not been a great problem in the "two-party" system because the other candidates usually received only a small percentage of the votes. But this new way of voting was more fair to all the candidates and to all those who voted.

What made the biggest difference was what Ward had first learned in that course in college. The vote for president not only gave the voters a second and third choice, but those choices were also ranked. In this final vote, a first place vote gave the candidate five points. A second choice vote gave the candidate three points. A third place vote gave the candidate one point. The candidate with the highest point total would become president and the candidate with the second highest number of points would become vice president. In this way, the voters had a much greater say in determining the next administration. This was a greater example of "government by the people." It was now that the people would even choose the vice president. That office would no longer be picked by the person and party of a presidential nominee.

When the day for the final vote arrived, Ward and Lisa went to vote. Ward teased Lisa by asking, "Are you going to tell me how you will be voting?"

Lisa laughed a little and then thought for a few seconds. "Oh, I haven't decided yet, but I probably will vote for people with names that I like. I have my secret sheet right here."

Because this election had ten choices and voters needed to vote for three in order of their preference, voters had been encouraged to examine the booklet of resumes and write down how they intended to vote. Once again, voters needed to vote for the three choices in order for their ballot to be valid.

Ward just smiled and squeezed Lisa's hand as they entered the building and got in line to receive their ballots. Because they both had followed the government suggestion to be prepared before voting, the actual time of filling in the three circles denoting their choices went quickly. They both had done the same regarding the vote for a new congressperson. They smiled at people on their way out, but didn't say any words to them.

Chapter 7:
"The Waiting Game"

Later that evening Ward and Lisa were invited to Dennis' home with a few friends. Without the two-party system, the "victory parties" for all ten candidates were similar in size: "just a few friends." There were more people than had been at the Ward and Lisa home for the regional vote. Dennis had wanted to share the evening with a few of his close friends, and so he offered his larger home for this event.

Other guests arrived slowly because it would be at least a couple of hours before any projection of the election could be made. Ward's and Lisa's friends greeted them, mainly with "Good luck tonight," but there was little political conversation—just talk about family, health, and the weather.

It was somewhat different as Dennis' friends came. Dennis introduced each to Ward and Dennis' wife introduced them to Lisa. Those preliminaries were followed mainly by statements similar to "It is good to finally meet you. Dennis has talked about you at great lengths." Both Ward and Lisa thanked them for their kind words. They both became a little flushed with all of the compliments.

When everyone had arrived, Dennis gave a short welcoming speech to all present. He ended with a general remark about the new method of electing a new administration. "I now really know this new election process is not only a better way for the voters, but it has also worked well for my pastor and friend, Ward Anderson, and his wife Lisa." That brought applause and a few cheers.

Ward had not planned on this, but he thought he ought to say something. "Thank you, but time will tell if it has worked well for Lisa and me. Even if I am elected to either office, time will just take a little longer to determine if it will work well for us." Ward squeezed Lisa's hand. The only sign of nervousness on his part was that he never left her side. Lisa was happy to be his support. It also helped her to not show her own anxiety.

The evening seemed to drag on, although it really went more quickly because of the friendly conversation which was mostly without anything political except for the perfunctory "good luck" comments. Dennis was the first to interrupt that mood. "They are starting to show early returns." That got the attention of those present and they all began to move closer to the several television sets scattered around the downstairs of the house.

There were preliminary area projections which showed that Ward was leading in "First Choice," with a scattering of "Second" and "Third" choices. The other nine candidates had smaller shares of all "choices." Dennis broke into the conversation again. "That's a promising start. But it is only a start. It will be another two hours before we will have enough results to see what is happening. Remember, these figures contain our home region."

"Anyway," Ward added. "I don't believe in counting chickens before they hatch. There are yet a lot of eggs out there in the rest of the nation." There were a few other comments among the guests, but most agreed to play it "low key," although the excitement level among the guests had been raised somewhat. The conversation returned to the former subjects such as children, sports, gardens, and other news.

The next three hours were spent that way with conversations interrupted only by the serving of snacks and refreshments. There were also the periodic silences to listen to continuing updates. Some of the reports encouraged more optimism in the group, but there were also others that were not so favorable—especially as the results came from regions closer to the west coast.

Even before all of the votes (and the points) had been counted, all of the networks projected two winners. They said that Robert James from California and Ward Adamson from Indiana were almost tied. It seemed one of them would win the presidential spot and the other would become the vice president, but it was too close to predict which one would end with the highest number of points.

There was a lot of excitement in the house because of that projection. Ward and Lisa were silent. They had a difficult time believing the news because they knew it was only a projection. Such projections had improved greatly over the years, but there was yet the possibility of error.

Chapter 8:
"The Fat Lady Sang"

It finally was over, but Ward started to believe it was only a beginning; or, maybe it was a dream and he would wake up soon. The final points vote was in. Robert James had the most "first choice" votes. Ward had won second place in that "pure vote," but neither had received a majority of votes. It was in "second" and "third" choices that Ward had risen above Robert in points. Ward had received enough more than Robert in those two areas to overcome his second place finish in the "first choice" vote. If Robert had received a majority of the vote, he would have become president. But, with the new process, the voters had spoken. With ten possible candidates, the voters had shown that a majority preferred Ward over Robert. The point system clearly showed that preference.

It was late in the evening and some of the guests had left earlier because they had to get up early for their jobs. Those who remained were excited and humbled by the results. The excitement was quite loud and active. Ward's supporters had difficulty controlling their joy and their surprise.

Ward and Lisa hugged quietly, just whispering words of love to each other, until the excitement moved toward them. "Well," Ward's first words came out with tears in his eyes, "the waiting is over."

Lisa gave Ward a kiss and whispered in his ear, "Congratulations, Mr. President." Then she hugged him again before the people gathered around them to give their congratulations. In a very short time, all but Ward and Lisa returned to their own homes.

When it quieted, Ward and the hosts were left alone. Dennis gave Lisa a hug and then bowed before Ward before he spoke. "Well, Mr. President, Now your real work begins. Just tell me how I can continue to help you in getting started."

"Let's take a couple of days off. We all need some rest. But, I think I might try to call Robert. It is a little earlier out there and I do have his number. I would like to congratulate him and tell him we will get together soon. I do want to make this a unified administration."

Dennis agreed and led him to a phone in his home office for privacy. Ward dialed and got an answer within a few rings. "I hope I have not awakened you, Bob, but I wanted to congratulate you, Mr. Vice President."

"I appreciate the call from you. I should have called you first, Mr. President, but I hesitated because of the time difference. My congratulations go to you."

"Oh, we stayed up until the end. It has been an interesting time. But, I also wanted to ask you how soon we can get together and plan for our administration. I want you involved from the start."

"Thank you. I appreciate your willingness. From the little I know about you, I think we will get along very nicely."

Plans were made to meet the following week in California. Ward had told him what he had always done in similar, planning situations—that Robert write down his ideas, questions, thoughts, and Ward would do the same before they met. That would make their meeting more beneficial. Then, the short conversation was ended. Ward and Lisa thanked their host for all that they had done. They went home much later than ever before.

They got ready for bed, kissed each other, and turned out the light. In a few minutes both turned toward each other and Ward put his arm around Lisa as she cuddled close to him. They both were tired, but not able to go to sleep. So, they didn't.

Chapter 9:
"Next Stop: The White House"

They had slept soundly, and it was late when they were awakened by the telephone. It was their eldest child. He offered his congratulations. The next hour allowed for many other calls, and it was noon before they decided to stop the calls and have lunch.

In the afternoon, Ward went to his office to begin making arrangements for resigning as Pastor of Grace Lutheran Church. That took more time than he thought because staff members were there. That necessitated a short staff meeting which was interrupted by a call from the bishop arranging for a brief meeting with Ward to plan for his exit procedure. Within a few days, Ward would no longer be pastor of the congregation. He would then only be President-Elect of the United States of America.

Before that time, Ward and the bishop had dated his resignation to begin on December first. His last work day would be on November 30—a Sunday, the time for Ward to preach his last sermon.

Even though everything had moved so quickly, Ward and Lisa had talked about that day during the time preceding the final vote. It was done in general terms because they both knew he had only one chance in ten, but just thinking about it had planted a few seeds in his mind.

It was to be "business as usual" with the regular schedule of the three morning worship services plus the one class-time for Christian education. Now, however, the staff was adding an evening "Farewell Party," to which both Ward and Lisa agreed. There needed to be a time to say "Goodbye."

When November 30 arrived, Ward was prepared—although anxious—for his last sermon. Everything went as normally planned, with an assistant conducting much of the liturgy, as was the usual procedure. Following the reading of the Gospel Text, the people sat and Ward was in the pulpit.

He paused for a few moments, looking over the "over-flow" crowd for the last time. Then he began:

"We have got to stop meeting like this." The congregation laughed, but there were tears in many eyes. Actually, Ward had begun that way because he hoped it would remove some of the tension in his own body. The laughter did help him and he then continued. "Today is Christ the King Sunday. It is now the end of another liturgical church year. Next Sunday we again start another new church year, as Christians around the world use that season of Advent to prepare for the celebration of the birth of God's Son on this earth.

"As with life itself, there is a cyclic pattern to what we experience on this earth. There are continuous times of ending and starting—of birth and death; of sinning and forgiving; of receiving and giving. Today, let me take you back in history over two millennia—back to the ancient city of Athens, Greece.

"Walk with me through those streets and look around. There are people in those same streets: children, and old men, and old women. But there are no young men. That segment of the population is in the Greek army, and they are far away from home. They are at war. They are risking their lives in order that their families might live in safety.

"But, the people we see on those streets are not smiling. They are worried. They are afraid. They are concerned about the future; worried if they even have a future; wondering if they will even have a life.

"But, as we walk further, we see a man running toward us. When he gets closer he begins to shout: 'The army has been victorious in battle! Don't be afraid! The army has saved you!'

"People began to gather around that runner. They begin to smile. There are shouts of joy from the crowd. There are prayers of thanksgiving to their gods.

"Now, come back to this day of our Lord. Come to the present time and apply what that history has to say to us.

"In the Greek language, that runner was called an 'Evangelist' and the message of victory he brought was named in Greek, the 'Evangeleon.'

"When the New Testament was written in the Greek, the authors talked about all that God had done for us by God's Son. When they wondered what Greek word they could use to convey that work of God in saving us through the death and resurrection of the Son of God, 'evangeleon' was the word they chose.

"Remember, the people in Athens had not done anything to bring about their safety—their victory over their enemies. The army did it. The same is true is the battle against sin and death and devil: the Son of God—Jesus, the Christ—did it for us. We did nothing but receive it. To describe that work— that gift—of God, we use words like 'grace,' 'love,' 'forgiveness,' 'salvation,' 'eternal life,' 'good news,' and 'gospel'—which is the Latin translation of the Greek word, 'evangeleon.'

"Now, then, although there is nothing we can do to obtain that unbelievable gift, our God-given responsibility is to show God our gratitude for the priceless and eternal gift. We show gratitude by doing all that God would have us do. That is the purpose of God's Law, just as it is the rules you set for your own children.

"I struggled for years to come up with some 'down to earth' example that would inspire and motivate followers of God to work for God by serving people on earth. I think I have found such a simple parable. I call it 'The Liturgy of a Football Game.' I invite you once more to come with me again to my first visit to an NFL game.

"It was unlike any worship I had ever attended. Long before I went, I was informed that the offering is received first. In fact, one needs a reservation even to be able to give that offering of a substantial sum. At least it guaranteed me a seat during the service. The worship is so popular that there is always a full congregation.

"Anyway, the Temple was located at a place of great accessibility and adequate parking. Why, they even had ushers in the parking lot—to collect an additional fee for parking, I soon discovered. I wondered how that would work at my home congregation.

"There were a lot of people there when I arrived in the parking lot. It seemed that many were having some sort of Eucharistic meal in the parking lot—some were even burning offerings to the Great God of the Game.

"As I entered the Temple, I was amazed at its size. Never before had I been in such a house of worship: thousands of seats, more ushers than worshippers at home. I learned, though, that the ushers' interest was not so much in helping me, but that they made certain I did not sit in someone else's place. And, there were additional ushers who were handing out bulletins—again, for a price. But, after giving this third offering, I found my place—a rather hard pew; but, at least my vision wasn't blocked by a post, as was true of the seat of the person next to me. On top of that the janitor had not done a very good job of sweeping out the refuse from the previous worship service.

"I tried to ignore the trash and the odor and looked around. This was one of those new churches, with worship 'in the round.' It was easy to see the large, green altar in the center, where—I soon realized—people's lives would be halted or advanced. The Altar Guild was putting on the finishing touches (white lines and mysterious numbers—symbolic, no doubt) on the altar. Others must have been controlling the huge reredos at one end of the Temple—an intricate backdrop for worship. They also had lights that spelled out sentences, names, numbers; even some advertising—properly paid for, I was certain.

"Somewhere in that vast Temple a band began playing the prelude, and I noticed a lot of mini-skirted acolytes dancing around in some sort of pre-worship ritual. Finally, the opening hymn was sung by the congregation as the U.S. flag was spotlighted. Well, at least I knew the words and they only sang one verse, because there were no hymnals.

"The Invocation consisted of a line-up type of announcement of the participants in the day's worship service. Those with the most colorful robes were called 'athletes' and were even divided into two 'teams.' Those wearing white and black stripes were to be the priests who officiated.

"It was a strange form of worship, but somehow the whole congregation seemed to know exactly when and how to respond. I looked for directions in the bulletin I had purchased, but there was no real order of liturgy there, only a lot of advertising (for which a fee surely had been paid). Yet, the people all around me were well acquainted with the liturgy as they responded in unison with 'YEA' and 'BOO' and even a lot of applause. Various other chants arose from time to time—seemingly impromptu, yet always arousing other versicles and responses from various sections throughout the congregation. Sometimes the liturgy called for the waving of home-made banners.

"There was nothing mild about the worship service. Everyone seemed to participate. I didn't notice any bashfulness on the part of those attending. To the contrary, there was even quite a bit of 'sharing the peace'—at least that is what it looked like to me.

"From time to time the action on the altar would stop. One of the priests would run out to the center of the altar and give some strange 'signs of the cross' which would bring additional liturgical responses from the congregation. At other times—during a lull in the service—people would leave their seats and soon return. One of the reasons for that was obvious because of the length of the service. But an additional reason seemed to be some kind of private communion, perhaps at one of the small chapels located around the main nave because people returned yet chewing on the elements.

"When the service was finally over, some of the congregation gave a great cheer, and a few of them rushed down to the altar. They began collecting various items used in the service: some sort of holy relics or reserved host, no doubt. I guess they were not supposed to do that because they were quickly removed from there by Assisting Ministers.

"Then, on my way home, everyone joined in the recessional hymn and postlude by tooting their automobile horns—a fitting benediction to such an unusual worship service.

"At home, I thought about the complete dedication of those worshippers: such commitment, such enthusiasm, such a crowd of people coming together each week to worship the God of the Game, and paying dearly for the privilege. Such Faith! If only Christians—in gratitude to God for the free gift of salvation—would only imitate it!

"Amen!"

There was a brief silence when Ward had finished. Then, one man stood up and shouted his response: "Amen!" Immediately, people throughout the church followed suit. The meaning of the word "Amen" is "I agree." That was the congregation's response to their long-time pastor on his last sermon. And then there was a loud and continuous applause from a standing congregation. Such response was most unusual from Lutherans, but the sermon and the occasion prompted them.

After a few moments, Ward faced the congregation again to quiet them and comment. "I thank you for that surprise, but I would direct it to my Lord and yours. Christ is my King and your King. It is because of all that he has done for us and to us that we trust him and obey him. His sacrificial suffering, death, and resurrection bring us our forgiveness and our life here and hereafter."

The service continued until the final hymn. It was then that Ward spoke again. "I leave you with a special hymn today. It is printed in the bulletin, and we will sing it to a very familiar tune. I wrote this hymn as a parting gift for you. It is my creed—what I believe about God and God's wishes. I have served you as your pastor following that faith. I leave you to serve this nation as its president, following that same faith."

"CREDO"
By The Rev. Ward Adamson

I BELIEVE IN GOD—THE FATHER; JESUS—SON; AND SPIRIT, TOO.
I BELIEVE THAT GOD CREATED, SAVED ME, AND WILL LIFE RENEW.
JESUS IS TRUE GOD, YET HUMAN—JUST LIKE I, YET WITHOUT SIN.
HE DELIVERED ME FROM SATAN—COMES AGAIN TO LIVE WITHIN.

I BELIEVE GOD'S KINGDOM'S PRESENT HERE AND NOW AMONG US TRUE.
I BELIEVE THAT I'M A MEMBER, CALLED AND BAPTIZED, STRENGTHENED, TOO.
GOD'S COMMANDMENTS ARE MY GUIDELINES HOW TO LIVE WHILE HERE BELOW.
OUR LORD'S SUPPER GIVES HIS PRESENCE TO ENABLE ME TO GROW.
I BELIEVE THAT GOD YET WANTS ME TO HELP BUILD A HEAV'N ON EARTH.
I BELIEVE THE HOLY SPIRIT COMES TO ME FOR SECOND BIRTH
TO URGE JUSTICE, FEED THE HUNGRY, STOPPING WARS THROUGHOUT THIS SPHERE.
CHRISTIANS ARE TO LEAD THE CHANGES TO GOD'S WISH FOR LOVE RIGHT HERE.

The service then ended with the versicle from Pastor Adamson—"Go in peace! Serve the Lord!" That was followed by the congregation's loud response—"Thanks be to God!"

Basically, there was similar, "overflow" attendance at the next two worship services; also the ending applause. During the education time, all classes met in the worship center for a "closing" time with their pastor. Ward gave a short, positive goodbye to them and closed with a prayer. All that was left was a late-afternoon program and buffet before the final goodbyes and good lucks.

At that final gathering and program, Ward and Lisa were praised and applauded for their thirty-plus years at Grace Lutheran Church. After receiving several "Farewell Gifts," Lisa spoke first. "I don't know what to say except to thank all of you for your faithfulness to your Lord and King on this special Sunday. In addition to that, I thank you for your love and support of me and my family for all of these years with you.

"It is difficult for us to leave......and....." the tears began to come. She wiped them and then continued. "I just want to let you know how much we love all of you and this congregation and this city. As we leave here and go to something entirely new, we do so with a great deal of anxiety. But we also go believing that God has been a big part of this decision. God goes with us even as God and our love remain with you."

Lisa choked up again, cried some more, decided she had said all that she could, and sat down. Women from the congregation rose from their seats first as they applauded and the rest of the people followed suit. Lisa wiped tears from her eyes, stood for a moment, and then sat again.

When the applause slowed, Dennis came to the microphone and the room became quiet again. Everyone could see that Dennis, also, had tears in his eyes. He wiped them briefly with his handkerchief and then began. "I have a confession to make, and I hope that all will forgive me. It seems that I am the person responsible for this sad—yet hopeful—day. This past year, I was the one who suggested to Pastor Adamson that he would make a good President of these United States. That request has proven to be prophetic. I also believe it was approved by God. I continue to pray it will also be blessed by God—at least for the next six years.

"It is now my pleasure to turn the rest of this evening over to the Reverend Ward Adamson: my pastor, my friend, my President-Elect of the United States of America."

All rose, applauded, whistled, shouted as Ward walked to the mike, hugged Dennis, and motioned for the people to sit again. He paused for a few moments while his eyes moved from side to side remembering his history with the people. Then he began.

"The Bible does speak to us about many times that are filled with God's love and God's plans. It was in such a fullness of time that God led the chosen people out of the slavery and death in Egypt. It was in the fullness of time that God took on life on this earth, and finally decided that the Son of Man and God needed to be sacrificed for human sin and rebellion. It was in such a fullness of time that God converted one Saul of Tarsus into a St. Paul who clarified the meaning of that gospel. It was in another fullness of time—when

Christ's Church had been corrupted—that God called Martin Luther into a reforming service.

"While I would not want to put myself into such an outstanding group of saints, I have to tell you that I would not be in this position today if I did not believe all of this is in agreement with God's wishes for this nation and world. I do believe that with all of my mind, even as I also believe that God was behind and with and leading the voters as they brought about a great change in our government—a change that made it possible that an unknown pastor from Indianapolis, Indiana, could become president of this nation.

"While I pray that God will help me in the work ahead, I also pray for this congregation. Let me assure you that following my love of God, my wife, and my family, this congregation is next in that line of priorities. I owe so very much to all of you.

"As to the details for your future as a congregation, it will be in good hands. The bishop 's office has made arrangements for a full-time, trained and accredited interim pastor to lead you through the next year or two as you plan for a new future here. It will not be rushed. It will be thorough. It will be spirit led. It will engage all of you in decision making. It will be successful.

"Lisa and I will be busy for the next six years. After that we have made no plans. We do not know the what or the where of our lives after Washington D.C. We do know we have made arrangements for renting our present home until we are close to the end of my term. Whether we return to it or not is presently not in our thoughts.

"Please be assured that this congregation will continue to be in our prayers as I know we—and this nation—will be in yours. We have been through much together, all under the care of a loving God.

"In closing, I can only say, goodbye, hoping you realize the salutation is a contraction of the original 'God be with ye.' That is our present word to all of you: 'God be with ye!'"

Ward moved back to Lisa and gave her a kiss as all of the people rose and applauded and cheered—most all of them with tears in their eyes and a heavy (but appreciative) heart.

Two days later, Ward met with Dennis to talk a little about a transition team. A few ideas were presented, some names were written down as possibilities, and then they moved on with a general discussion concerning the Cabinet.

With the new method of election, there was no need—as in the past—to "reward" the highest financial contributors with Cabinet positions. Instead, Ward suggested they merely write down some names that the transition team would contact to see if they were interested in becoming a part of the new administration. If there was interest, the next step would be interviews.

Ward and Dennis talked about the time Ward had been interviewed before he was called to be the pastor. Ward quickly said that the call process in the church had many flaws, and he had a better way of doing it.

What had been done in the church was that any pastor desiring to be called to a congregation—whether it was the first time or simply the desire to move to another church—would fill out a form telling things about himself or herself. Those congregations needing a pastor did the same kind of self-study. The bishop then tried to match up a congregation's needs with some pastor's quality. The pastor the bishop picked would then be sent for an interview.

The problem with that system was two-fold. First of all, the pastor wrote his own evaluation, and it was seldom accurately done. Ward told of one instance that had happened in a neighboring congregation. The named candidate had listed his strengths as being a worship and evangelism leader. But, when the committee checked the records from that pastor's present congregation, they showed that—in the past five years—the congregation had declined both in worship attendance and total membership. Those were the two areas the candidate said were his strengths. He had lied on his report.

Ward told Dennis that a joke among pastors was every pastor should tell a congregation their strengths were youth work and the ability to raise money. The joke was that, although both items were most often what congregations wanted, very few pastors knew anything about young people or raising money.

The second flaw in the process was that the candidate was most often given a copy of the congregation's self-study. Therefore he or she knew what the congregation wanted. It was simply a matter of telling the congregational committee what they wanted to hear.

Ward said, "We will not make those mistakes. Anyway, basically what we will look for in Cabinet members will be good morals, intelligence, and ability to lead and motive people, just like excellent CEOs." Pointing at Dennis he continued, "Someone like you. And that brings me to a question. Will you be my Chief of Staff?"

Dennis laughed. "I know the political climate in Washington has changed for the better, but I don't think my talents fit in with the role you suggest. I would think the first person you should interview for Chief of Staff would be the present one. He seems to have served very well. The nation and your administration might profit a great deal with keeping some of the present staff leaders, at least for a while. If they don't want to stay or don't fit in, you can always bring in new people."

"That does make sense," Ward replied, hoping he wasn't showing disappointment that the closeness of working with Dennis would be coming to an end. Then he continued. "I also intend of giving everyone a quick Myers/Briggs personality program. I have used that for my entire ministry and have high hopes that it will assist us in forming the administration. The reason for doing it is it reveals a lot of different qualities in each person: qualities that are essential to know in developing good working relationships.

"I became very convinced of that in using Myers/Briggs in many different ways in my pastoral work. I used it with couples in both pre-marital counseling and helping problem marriages. I used it to place elected persons as council committee heads so that everyone was working in areas that suited their talents and their desires. I used it in the formation of committees formed for short-term purposes.

"Years ago, when we were planning to celebrate the congregation's twenty-fifth anniversary, I invited volunteers to meet and help with the planning. About fifteen people showed up, and the first thing I did was a quick Myers/Briggs assessment of each person.

"My only purpose for that assessment was to find out how each person viewed time. Myers/Briggs can tell me whether a person deals mainly in the past, the present, the future, or, if they deal well in all three time periods. Then, when I checked the results, I assigned the two people who were 'past time' related to work on the celebration committee and develop a brochure reminding members of our history.

"When we met the next week, both of those persons came with stacks of old church newsletters, bulletins, newspaper clippings, and photos—an amazing collection from each, because they were both 'past time' related, and they had saved historical items of the congregation. It was also interesting that one of them was a librarian. Myers/Briggs was right on the money.

"Those persons who were 'present time' people I asked to form a committee to help us have a party to celebrate where we were now. The people who were 'future time' related I gave the responsibility to develop something for the congregation to point us forward in our mission. The two people who turned out to live equally well in all three time periods I asked to be co-chairs of the entire committee.

"I think such a method made our entire celebration an excellent time. I am convinced it can make this administration one of the best ever."

"I remember that anniversary and commented to others about how well it was organized, but I didn't know how you did it. That is one of the best ideas I have heard in a long time." Dennis was shaking his head in agreement. "I'll keep it in mind and see if I can find a way to use it in my business, maybe start with my board of directors. I would like to have you handle it for me, but you are going to be quite busy for the next six years."

Ward smiled. "I'm glad you like it. There are many other people trained as presenters of the program, so you should have no problem getting a good leader. Incidentally, there are other personality items that also show up. There are people who want to make instant decisions and those who want to discuss it longer. Just knowing that is the case can ease tension within any group that uses discussions before decisions. It can also be helpful to know that you have both kinds of personalities involved. If all members are the same personality type, you can make decisions that are not thought out enough, or you can discuss something to death and never make a decision until it is too late."

Dennis again shook his head in amazement. "How did I manage all these years without knowing and doing those things?"

"It's because you instinctively knew and used a lot of it," Ward interjected. "Maybe God was also speaking to you and leading you to do what was right."

"You do have a way to remind all of us how dependent we are upon God's loving kindness." Ward was again shaking his head in agreement.

They spent about another hour writing down ideas and names. It was exciting for both Ward and Dennis. There was also an aura of disbelief in their discussion. They had talked a lot previously about the tremendous odds against what had happened to them. They were also anxious about how the future would unfold. But, they knew if they worked as though everything depended upon them and prayed as though everything depended upon God it would all happen for the good of the nation and the world. Both would become better.

The meeting with the vice president took place at Robert's home in California. Ward had made that choice. He did not want to give Bob any idea that the next six years would be filled with instances where the vice president always had to come to the president. Ward wanted to show a little reciprocity.

Besides that, Ward was interested in spending a few days in a warmer climate. He also wanted to give Lisa a little different environment, brief as it would be. Lisa could also meet Bob's wife and they could have their own discussion about how their personal and governmental relationship might develop. After all, neither of them had ever been in this kind of situation before.

Ward brought along several papers filled with names and ideas. He first, however, wanted to listen to what Bob had written. Again, listening first was the good habit Ward had developed.

A big change for the presidential couple was the addition of Secret Service people accompanying them on the trip. They would have to get used to that, but it was a strange experience.

Things had changed over the decades because the world and the nation had changed, and a lot of it was not good. Too many people thought the answer to their problems was simply to shoot someone, and the president would make a good target. Gone were the days which President Truman faced. Ward remembered the story about him which the political science professor had told them. It passed through his mind again because it was such a good example of the change.

It had been the story that Truman did not have Secret Service protection; he did not have a presidential retirement; he turned down any use of his presidential career for personal gain.

Little by little, that entire atmosphere changed as politicians acquired power and money—mainly because of the absence of term limits and the degrading of the political scene and process which removed government from the people and gave it to the top one percent.

It had gotten so bad and so ingrained that no one was able to amend it, much less to stop it. Every politician seeking election to Washington promised that they would work to change how the U.S. government worked. But, like a southern governor decades ago who had made the same promise—and believed it himself—he fell in with the rest and became the worst governor that state had ever experienced. The same was even truer in the national capitol.

After decades of such arrogance, the people finally rose up and got changes made at the congressional level. It began as voters organized and forced politicians seeking election or re-election to sign a legal document pledging that they would introduce and vote for term limits in Congress. Further, they signed that they would not ever seek re-election following their present term. If they signed that document, the voters would support the candidate. If they refused to sign, the voters supported and elected other candidates. If—after they were elected—they failed in that formal and legal written agreement, they were subject to serve one year in prison.

It took a great deal of "arm twisting," but year by year the make-up of Congress changed until there were enough votes in Congress also to change the process to a better way to nominate and elect a president. That change had been passed three years earlier. Ward and Bob were the first administration to finally be elected according to the wishes of the voters.

Now, the two of them were engaged in a discussion concerning the way to form a new administration. Although Ward's position would be above Bob's, Ward was interested in elevating the role of the vice presidency. This first meeting did a great deal to accomplish that goal, and Bob was most appreciative. When the meeting ended and all the decisions had been made, he shook Ward's hand and commented, "This meeting was great. Thank you for including me. I was a little disappointed when I saw you had overtaken me. But I now know this will be an exciting and fruitful term for a vice president. I will have you to thank for the experience."

Ward and Bob ended their meeting and went to find their wives. They had finished their "government" discussion some time earlier and were just enjoying each other's company and getting better acquainted.

"Well, what are you two doing?" was Ward's question.

Bob's wife, Betty, answered first. "After solving all of the problems the two of you will face, we are just having a girl's talk. You have a marvelous wife, Mr. President. I was wondering what I would be doing for the next six years, but Lisa has talked about several ideas for me. I think I will really enjoy what we have talked about doing as Mrs. One and Two."

They all laughed about those titles. Bob spoke first. "I am so glad you two are getting along so well. I think the same could be said about Ward and me. I'm sorry. I mean about Mr. President and me."

"Bob, I think you and I need to develop the practice of using our first names when we are alone."

"I serve at the pleasure of the president and the voters, so I will do what you suggest, Ward."

They spent the rest of the day in getting better acquainted, talking mainly about family, travel, former occupations, and whatever came to mind. After dinner, Ward and Lisa left for their hotel. The next day they would be flying to Washington. The transition office was ready to be open, and Dennis had agreed to meet them there and set up that office. Lisa was invited to the White House to see the living quarters and think about what they might want to change before they moved in. That proved to be an exciting idea for her. She had never given any thought to the idea that she might one day be living in the White House. She could only think that "God works in mysterious ways."

BOOK FOUR

Chapter 1:
"Let the Games Begin"

W ard and Dennis started to organize the transition team staff. Because there was no longer any kind of "Party System," they both agreed they would use many of the available people who had worked for the previous administration. Some of that staff had moved into other jobs, but it was decided to give the other persons the opportunity to earn a place with the new administration. All those who were hired were told of that possibility, depending upon the quality of their work on the transition team.

Dennis informed Ward that he would be available in Washington for only three days due to demands of his business. But, he explained, as he introduced another man to Ward, "This is George Schultz. He has been the organizational planner for my business for quite a few years, and he is really good at organizational designing. He will head this transitional staff as long as you need him."

After a brief greeting, they all sat down and got to work. It was only minutes into the discussion that Ward understood the truth of Dennis' recommendation. George's suggestions and ideas were succinct and appropriate. They quickly completed their initial planning and began assignments to those who had worked the process before. They also discovered they would not need very many additional persons because those they had seemed eager to impress the new president.

While the others went to start their assigned work, Ward, Dennis, and George began to talk about the White House staff. Because word got around that this new president might wish to retain some former staff members, Ward had already received some inquiries from members of the present staff; so they talked about times and ways to interview them for possible jobs. Again, because of the end of the "party system," it would be possible to retain many people without worrying about "party loyalty."

Ward was worried only about one thing. "What about the fact that all of these people have worked in the former system? Is that going to be a problem for us down the road?" he asked.

George responded: "I had not thought about that. It is possible that some of them have connections with former lobbyists or others who might try to buy their 'influence' regarding this new administration. I guess we can simply play along with it for a while and critique the performance and bias of each on our staff. We can also make it clear to all that we will not tolerate any underhanded shenanigans."

"I'll go along with that," Ward said after a few moments of silent thinking. "And I have also added to my method a new policy. I have been in the 'forgiveness business' for thirty years because that is the major overall umbrella of the Christian religion. But, this is a different 'business.' I had thought—through the years—that government management should have a 'one strike' policy. We can make that known immediately to everyone who works for this administration. We can forgive someone, but this government belongs to the people, and no one will be an exception to the 'one strike rule.'"

George nodded his agreement. "I do not have any problem with that at all."

George then wrote down the many items he would oversee in the transition, and then they talked about the inauguration day events. While the actual inauguration program was fairly well set—except for the new president's speech—Ward did have a suggestion for the Inauguration Ball. "You will notice I said that in the singular. I think the government should schedule only one ball. If there are other groups that want to have their own ball to celebrate, let them plan and pay for it themselves. Further, the one Inauguration Ball would be the only one that the presidential party would attend."

"Are you sure about that?" asked Dennis. "I can imagine a lot of Washington would not be happy with that."

"I might be convinced otherwise, but I want the voters and Congress to know that my administration will be different right from the start. Again, there can be a lot of other balls, but let those who want them plan and pay for them themselves. I suppose we could secretly also make plans for a quick visit to a couple of them, if that would help appease the disappointment."

Dennis thought a bit and then responded, "I think it might work out that way. All the people who want to come to the ball can't all fit in one place, anyway."

Ward went on. "My idea for the 'official' ball is to limit it to one thousand people. That would include everyone elected to Congress, and spouse or friend. In addition there would be people from the White House staff and the members of the Cabinet. Also, we need to count family and some friends of the president and vice president. We would need to get the news and the invitations out as soon as we can so other people can make their own arrangements to reserve a proper place, entertainment, and so forth."

There were a couple more comments, but the idea was decided. Preliminary planning was assigned to a member of the team. There also needed to be an advance notice of the reasoning behind the decision, especially noting the frugality that should be expected from this new administration, including the concept that savings in such things would be better spent "helping people."

"Dennis had told me a lot about you and your philosophy of life, but I did wonder some concerning how much of it was true." George was smiling as he said it. "If you continue in the same way, Mr. President, this will be a great six years for a lot of people in the world."

"Well, thank you, George. But, be careful with the compliments. Humility is a struggle for me. However, I feel that same way about Dennis, and I have known him for over thirty years. I have always been surprised by him, but never disappointed."

The next two days were spent in more details in planning. Ward wanted to get Dennis' ideas on the table before he had to leave for his company business. After that, George and Ward would be joined by the vice president elect as they continued their tasks until after the inauguration.

In the days that followed, Ward personally talked with the present chief of staff to see if it would work for him to continue in the new administration. After a short time, Ward was satisfied enough to ask Chief of Staff Ronald Albright if he would be willing to take a quick Myers/Briggs Personality typing. Ron agreed, but added, "I took that a few years ago. I can tell you I am an ESTJ."

Ward smiled. Any doubts about how well Ron and he could work together were answered. He had wanted someone who was a thinker—as was Ward—and here he was. He had the experience. He had the knowledge. He was what Ward wanted. "Will you continue as my chief of staff?"

"I would love to do that. I have followed your campaign and think we would work well together."

"Only one more thing," Ward interjected. "I do not want a 'Yes Man.' Will you be able to always be honest with me about your thoughts—to disagree openly with me, when that is the situation?"

"Because you are also an ESTJ, you ought to know that I will."

"Then, the job is yours, if you accept it."

"I am happy to accept it, Mr. President. I hope I do a very good job for you."

"Ron, I am certain you will. Thank you for accepting. Now, while you do not work for me yet, I would ask you to write down the names of those heads of each department that you would recommend for us to interview with the possibility that they might also choose to remain. I would have the final say in that, but I want your input before I start on it myself."

"Will tomorrow be okay for the list?"

"Yes, indeed."

The transition team did its job well. As the date for inauguration neared, all of the publicity had been released and all arrangements for the day completed. There had been only one small problem. One senator had called in his reservation for the official ball with the statement that there would be eight people in his party. He was politely, but firmly, informed that there would be only two in his party. He began to argue with the person in charge, telling him who he was and he needed those eight reservations. The response was again that the limit was two—one for him and one for his wife. He was not happy with that, but his only other choice was to attend one of the unofficial balls that various groups had scheduled. He finally consented to the two reservations, with the notation that he would be having a talk with the new president. The worker made a note of the conversation and passed it on to his supervisor.

Chapter 2:
"The Beginning of the New Experiment"

While weather is always a question mark—especially in January—the sun came out in all its glory and the wind was non-existent. People hoped the wonderful weather was an omen for the new administration and for the nation. The change to this better way of electing national government was now complete. Although there were a few lawyers and some wealthy people in places of power, every one of them knew they were only there for six years. That was not enough time for any to become entrenched with a great deal of power. Added to that was the elimination of any political party which demanded their allegiance. Further, the outlawing of lobbyists meant the absence of power and money groups which could buy government preference from individual members of Congress. Any variance to the rule would result in expulsion from Congress and a jail sentence. For the first time in U.S. history, each elected person was subject only to the voters and to the welfare of the nation.

It was early in the morning that Ward and Lisa awoke to their alarm. Ward reached over to shut off the buzzing and then gave Lisa his usual morning kiss. She responded with a firm hug, telling him, "Well, this is your last day of freedom. Tomorrow you belong to this nation. Here is a 'good luck kiss.'"

Ward eagerly responded to that, increased his hug, and then—slowly—released her from his embrace. "We had better get up before we forget and don't get up." They were expecting their entire family in a couple hours. They would all be coming to join them in the caravan for the day, in that procession of security personnel and vehicles which would now become their normal manner of city transportation.

When the family had all arrived, there were the usual greetings between parents and children and grandchildren—all dressed in their "Sunday Best." Within a few minutes the line of vehicles moved out and took them to St. John

Episcopal Church, where they would all attend the traditional "Morning Prayer Service" which had begun with President Washington. When they left the church, the Secret Service ushered them back into the vehicles for the next stop.

When they arrived at the Capitol, they had some time before they were ushered out to the platform where the inauguration ceremony was to take place. During that time, Lisa kept her hand in Ward's, gripping it as if she believed she was about to lose her husband to the nation. Ward sensed that. He took her in his arms and kissed her, whispering, "I'm always yours, Lisa. You are more important to me than being president." Lisa smiled and relaxed her grip. It was time to go out to the crowd.

After Ward and Bob had been sworn in by the Chief Justice of the Supreme Court, Ward walked to the podium, accompanied by a tremendous roar of the crowd. He smiled and waved to the crowd as his face turned somewhat red. While he always liked to be appreciated, he yet had a slight problem handling compliments. It was only a few moments before he raised his arms and began to silence the crowd. The people reluctantly quieted and Ward grabbed the podium with both hands. He looked out over this new, immense "congregation," took a deep breath, and began.

After the necessary greetings to important people on the platform, he turned back to the crowd and concluded with "…and you, the people of this great nation." Then he began his inauguration address.

"It was several generations ago that President John F. Kennedy challenged the citizens of this nation with the words: 'Ask not what your country can do for you, but what you can do for your country.' I am here today as proof that you took those words to heart. You—the people of this nation—started the process that did a great favor to this country. You—the people of this nation—worked and protested and persevered to change what was wrong with this government and culture. You—the people of this nation—fought the good fight to change our political process closer to what our Founding Fathers had envisioned. You—the people of this nation—have returned us to a government truly of and by and for the people. I thank you for that."

He was interrupted at that point by a wave of applause, cheers, and shouts. When he quieted them down again after about a minute, Ward continued. "I am a living symbol of what all of you have accomplished. I stand here as proof that now 'anyone can become president of this nation.' I am not wealthy. I am not a lawyer. I am not in this position for more than six years. The same can be said for most of the members of the new Congress. You have elected all of us to govern for you and for your benefit.

"I hold on to my promise to you in the election process. I have selected some of the best minds in this country to assist me. I am grateful for their willingness to serve both me and you. But, I have also chosen people for this administration who are of differing personalities and differing styles, and even opposing views. I have done that because it is the way I have always managed.

I want to know both what is right about a plan and also what is wrong with it. It is the only correct way to find the truth.

"As I also promised, we will continue with our website that allows all of you to express your feelings and your complaints and your suggestions for the governing of your nation. We will continue to monitor that site. We will consider what is presented there. I do want to know what ideas are present among our citizens.

"I do not do these things in order to be re-elected. Every person in government can now do 'what is right, rather than what will get them re-elected.' What we have here in this government of these United States of America does not belong to elected officials. It belongs to all citizens."

Again, the crowd felt moved to show their agreement and appreciation for those words. It was a "new day," and the people were excited about it. So, they showed it. When it got quiet again, Ward concluded: "I welcome all of you to continue to be involved in the politics of this nation. Remember the root word for politics means 'of and by and for the people.' That means all of you. I will pray and work so that six years from now—when you will rejoice with a new President—you will also rejoice as you remember the job I will have completed by then. Until that time, let us all make this nation and this world a little more like 'Heaven on Earth'—where no one goes hungry, where everyone has shelter, where poverty will be eliminated, where implements of war will become tools for peace, where life will remain healthy.

"I thank you for the opportunity you have voted to give me. I thank God for this nation and for all of you. Now, we need to celebrate what you have accomplished. After that, I need to get to work.

"I close with a word that I have often used. It means 'I agree.' The word is: 'Amen.'" As he moved from the podium, the crowd quickly rose and gave their applause and cheers, many of them repeating "Amen."

Ward left the podium as the applause continued. When he was at Lisa's side, he gave her a hug and a kiss. Then he turned back to the crowd and waved for about a half a minute. At that point the podium crowd began greeting each other before they left. It had been a special moment in time within the history of the United States of America.

Chapter 3:
"Shall We Dance?"

To show that change would begin early in the new administration, the inaugural ball that evening was singular. Gone were the numerous locations of balls to accommodate all of the friends and supporters and government officials. The one inaugural ball location could handle one thousand people. That was the limit of invitations sent out. Ward submitted a list of those he and Bob wanted to come, limiting each to less than one hundred guests. The rest were chosen by a committee headed by Ward's chief of staff. It was a difficult—maybe, unpopular—decision in all respects, but Ward wanted economy from the very beginning. When questioned about it, he simply smiled and responded, "Economy begins at home and at the top. Those not invited can have their own parties at their own expense."

There were other surprises for those lucky enough to attend the official ball. The government paid only for the hall and the orchestra. All refreshments were "Dutch Treat." Dennis did pay for the champagne for the families of the new president and vice president, with assurance that the cost would not be a business or tax write-off. His toast was short and to the point. "May you both be blessed with faithfulness to your goals. May your work be successful and beneficial to this nation and the world. May what you do in the next six years verify the trust people have placed in you. May God bless you, this nation, and the world."

The evening was spent in joy, conversations, and acquaintance with leaders of Congress. Of course, there was a suitable amount of dancing and a lot of "congratulations." Ward and Lisa were at their congenial best, not giving much thought to the work and pressures which would begin tomorrow. Even so, Ward had to politely fend off the few people who wanted to turn the conversations toward government business. "Sorry, but I promised Lisa we would not talk business tonight. Let's just enjoy the evening."

Chapter 4:
"A New Administration"

While his staff worked on getting settled and organized in their White House responsibilities under the direction and supervision of Ronald Albright, the Chief of Staff, Ward had called together the new Cabinet for a late afternoon meeting. It was to be followed by dinner at the White House, and then a discussion and brainstorming session in the early part of the evening.

Ward was at the conference table early so he could personally greet and thank each member. When all were assembled just before the appointed time, Ward began the meeting. "Welcome to the next six years. I want to thank you all for being on time. I can fairly well assure you that we will always start on time. I always remember what the chair of one of the committees I was on said: 'Of course we will start on time. How else are those who are not yet here know they are late when they arrive?'"

He said that with a big smile—enough so that the Cabinet members laughed. The ice was broken. Ward proceeded with his opening remarks. "Chiefly, I thank you all again for accepting this great privilege and responsibility.

"In our interview with each of you, there was a lot of mutual learning. All of you were chosen because I believe you have a lot of the same dreams for this nation that I possess. I said 'a lot of the same dreams' because I do not want you to be 'Yes Men' or 'Yes Women.'

"You will remember that all of you took the Myers/Briggs Personality Typing Inventory. That means I now have a much better understanding of how each of you function. I have learned the major process by which each of you operate. I also now understand how each view time, and whether you think chiefly in past or present or future concepts. For your information, two of you beside me are equally comfortable dealing in all three time elements. All of that is good. It gives this illustrious group the variety I was seeking. Just remember that, although we are each somewhat different, none is worse or better than anyone else. There is an old statement of truth that 'God don't make no junk.'"

There were a lot smiles at that as people nodded and looked at each other. Then Ward continued. "Let's get to work."

"There are a few things I want each of you to begin thinking about, and, if worthwhile, planning how to implement them.

"Steve, as Attorney General, I want you to consider how our entire judicial system can be improved. I do not believe we presently, always, have 'equal justice under the law.' I also think the president should not be submitting a name for Congress to approve for Supreme Court Justice. I think that violates the concept of 'separation of powers.' For the same reason, I will not ever grant executive pardon for those whom courts have found guilty."

There were a lot of members again nodding in the affirmative, but no one spoke at this time. Ward continued. "Dianne, as Secretary of Defense, your overall concern needs to center itself on the notion of defense. We will work hard to change the willingness of national leaders to use war as a first option, but we also need to be prepared to defend ourselves. Defense is a part of the Constitution. I find it amusing that those words are in 'Section Eight,' but that's another idea. Luckily, with our advanced technology, we will be able to do defense with more efficiency and effectiveness, and with many less people. I want no 'Defense Initiative' concepts. We will defend, but we will not be the aggressors. There are other forms of diplomacy able to maintain peace in our world.

"Along with that, I want you and this whole cabinet to think about developing a program of service to our nation and the world for every citizen—either in the armed forces or in other social community service of many varieties. But, we need to reward those who serve. If we can keep the peace, all nations will save immense amounts of money that can be used in better ways than waging war.

"That is enough to begin for today. I will bring up other suggestions for each of you at our next meeting, Now, I welcome your ideas about what you have heard. We will discuss them for a while. Then we will go for dinner at the White House and forget about them. One of the values of the brain is to plant a seed idea, let it lie, and let the brain deal with it for a while. We will come back to it for a short time after dinner. So, what do you have to say?"

There was a real eagerness from the members to respond, some for and a few against. A secretary was taking notes so nothing would be lost in memory. After a while, Ward said, "Thank you all. That was a good start. Now we go for dinner. But, remember, no discussion about this until we return. Enjoy dinner. Enjoy conversation. Stop working for a while." Then all left and went to the White House to be greeted by the First Lady.

Shortly before the Cabinet members, their spouses had already arrived for the dinner. Lisa also served as hostess for them—greeting each with brief conversation and leading them into the room for cocktails. Very soon the

Cabinet members arrived and joined them. Ward also made it a point to get acquainted. This was a good test for his exceptional memory for names, a skill which had served him well as pastor of a large congregation. He hoped it would continue.

Lisa had previously—with a few suggestions from Ward—figured out a seating arrangement for the dinner. Husbands and wives were seated across the table from each other to facilitate a better mix for conversation. Also, every other seat was occupied by a non-Cabinet person. That had been one of Ward's suggestions. It was meant to help keep conversation away from members' thoughts about their first meeting, but also to increase the development of friendship among all present. Ward and Lisa followed suit.

After a brief cocktail "half-hour," Lisa continued as hostess. "Welcome again to all of you. Welcome to YOUR House. It IS your House, although my husband and I expect to live here for the next six years. This will be a very leisurely dinner. We hope you all enjoy yourselves and that we become much better acquainted. Before we begin, let us give thanks."

Lisa also led the "grace" with a very general, but very beautiful, prayer. Then she raised her glass with a toast. "To the future of this nation and the world! May peace and prosperity be the norm for all of earth's peoples and the earth itself." She sat down and the dinner began. It was a good time for all. The next two hours were filled with food and conversations—many varieties of each.

At the end, Ward stood and announced, "Cabinet members will return to the Conference Room until nine o'clock. During that time the First Lady will be giving the spouses a tour of the White House. She has an ulterior motive in doing that. She is glad to have both husbands and wives in the group. She will be taking notes on your comments, and she wants your suggestions as to making a few—I stress 'very few'," as he glanced across the table toward Lisa— "changes to our living quarters in this fine home you are providing us for the next few years."

With that, the dinner party split into two groups: Ward leading the Cabinet members back to finish the meeting, and Lisa gathering the spouses to begin the tour.

"We will adjourn exactly at nine pm," were Ward's opening words. "A lot of what we might say after that time most likely would be repetitious or of little value anyway. Just remember that this process does not allow any evaluating of previous ideas, no criticism and no applause. We want our brains to spill out any and all ideas that are within us. Who wants to begin the brainstorming?"

Steve Layton, the Attorney General, spoke first. "As a lawyer and former judge, I think my brain has been working silently overtime on your assignment to me earlier this evening. I was able to change gears during the dinner, but even on our walk here, it started me thinking. Maybe we need to think about proposing some changes or amendments to the U.S. Constitution."

"I have been thinking about that ever since the president asked me to consider membership on this Cabinet," Marilyn Lopez, Secretary of Interior, joined in. "Our Founding Fathers had no idea of guessing about the way in which this nation has developed. Our society is far different from the one in which they lived. There might be several ways to have changes that would fit our condition much better and much clearer."

There were additional comments relating to that subject. Members avoiding saying it was not a good idea. Instead, they did follow the rules of brainstorming with general ideas about changing the minds of those who might oppose "tampering" with the Constitution.

After about twenty minutes, when there was a lull in the conversation, Ward interjected. "We seem to have ended that topic for now. Who can offer something different?"

"Maybe this group could also give thought to what began earlier regarding our national defense," Roberta Flynn, the Secretary of Health and Human Services, asked, as she looked at Ward and also around the table. "How do we change the warring history of the whole world?"

Amos Johnson, Secretary of Veteran's Affairs, was quick to jump in. "Perhaps we have already begun that process in having Dianne as Defense Secretary. The general idea has been around for several generations that 'if mothers made decisions about sending their sons and daughters into battle, maybe we wouldn't have wars.'" Those at the table all smiled at that, including Ward, because he had believed in that possibility for a long time. That was why he was interested in having a woman in that Cabinet position.

"Adding to that thought," Edward Beyer, Secretary of Agriculture, spoke next. "We probably should concentrate on the causes of war. If we can lessen those issues, I think we would have a better chance of reaching that goal."

The Secretary of Education, Betty O'Donell, continued the process. "In addition to that, perhaps there is some way we can influence the language and concept of war itself. It has been so glorified in novels, movies, television, public opinion—not to mention children's toys." And so it continued. There seemed to be a realization that most of their dreams for nation and world depended greatly on the elimination of the waste and expense created by war. The room vibrated with the excitement of ideas presented. There seemed to be no end until Ward rose from his chair and announced, "It is now the end of our allotted time. Thank you all for you participation and partnership. My office will provide each of you with a transcript of our meeting. Read it over. Add any additional thoughts for future consideration. But, what has been spoken here is not for publication. We will give to the press a very general statement about our evening, but we do not want public discussion about what are only ideas. Silence about such things is a presidential order. Now, let's go back and reacquaint ourselves with our families." Thus did the first meeting of the new Cabinet end.

Ward and Lisa did the usual "farewells" and were finally on their way up to the residence. While in the elevator, Ward gave Lisa a kiss. "You were the perfect Hostess, Lisa, as I knew you would be."

"It was really a good feeling, although I was a little nervous at first. I wish I had your ability for remembering names, though. I'll have to study up on that."

"There will usually be someone to remind you of the names if you forget. Don't worry about it. I'll also help you with some of the tricks. You'll become a natural at it quite soon."

"Thanks, Ward. How did your first meeting go?"

"Very well. We got a lot of ideas out into the open with brainstorming. I need to write down a few things before we go to bed. It won't take long."

"I'm glad this first event is over and went so well. It was such a pleasant time at dinner without any political or business conversation. I'm glad you suggested it that way. It was so much better for all—especially the spouses."

As they left the elevator, Ward continued. "I was hoping it would work out like that. Most of these people are acquainted only by name and reputation. This evening was a good start at bonding."

In the residence, Lisa went to get ready to relax and watch the news before retiring. Ward stopped at a desk and made notes to himself, as well as a memo for his secretary. Tomorrow would be a full work day. Besides meeting with the heads of his administrative staff and bringing them on board with a few of his ideas, there was already a list of appointments with congressional leaders who were eager to get in some "browning" points with the new president. Ward wasn't eager to do that, except to get acquainted with them. He also hoped to surmise each one's position and personal agenda. After all, Congress made the laws.

After watching the news with Lisa and informing the switchboard that they were retiring, sleep came quickly to both of them. Their last words were, "I wonder if the phone will ring tonight."

Ward rose early the next day—that had been his custom for a long time. He went for a brisk walk, this time—unlike past years—accompanied by his assigned Secret Service guard. "This will take a while for me to get used to having you around for my morning walk," he told one of the men. He also made a mental note to see if there would be a way to diminish the size of all that protection. It just seemed to him to be too much waste—too many people, too many vehicles in presidential travel.

When he returned, Lisa was up and waiting for him for breakfast. "How was the walk? It does seem like it is going to be a fine day."

Ward gave her a kiss and answered, "My group walk was a new experience, and, yes, the weather is quite pleasant for this time of year. Of course, I don't really know how it is supposed to be in Washington now. Well, I'm off for a shower, this time without guards."

The breakfast was leisurely, a time to enjoy each other's company before the start of a very busy day. When they finished, Lisa went to meet with her personal secretary to plan ways in which she could productively spend her time in some form of public service. After all, she would no longer be involved in the life of a parish congregation. Ward went to the Oval Office for his eight am meeting with Ronald. That was followed by a meeting with the heads of each administrative department.

When all were present, Ward walked around the room greeting each. There were a couple of people whom he had not met before, but the others he had met at least once earlier. Then Ward sat down at his desk. "I wanted to meet all of you officially and to clarify for you my dreams and my values. The most important thing for you and the entire staff to remember is that I demand complete honesty in the work we all do. Any deviation from that will result in immediate dismissal. Enough said.

"My dream is what I have stated throughout the campaign and what has been and remains on my website. If any of you are not clear on that, you can easily refresh your memory.

"I want each of you to make both of those items clear to your entire staffs. At the same time, everyone working for each of you—as well as I—should be open to discuss the pros and cons of everything we do. I welcome dissenting arguments because we each could be wrong in our decisions. I promise you I will listen and consider opposing views, with the understanding that I make all final decisions.

"So, welcome to your work. My prayer is that this might be the most beneficial administration in our history.

"Now, we have about an hour to ask questions and learn answers. Anyone want to be first?"

The group sort of looked at each other, but no one spoke at first. The Chief of Staff broke the silence, "Mr. President, Jim Thomson is the new Press Secretary and he asked me about styles of reporting and answering questions from the press. Jim, now you have your chance to ask the president."

"I have a lot of experience in reporting, but this is a whole new thing for me. For example, if I know something, but I am informed that it is not yet to be reported, what exactly do I say?"

"Good question. It really applies to all of you and to your staff. There are basically two areas in that question.

"First, there are some issues that cannot be reported. For example, we often will only discuss ideas which we may eventually discard. And there are items related to national security. Oh, of course, there may be those things concerning personnel. In all those times we either report something like, 'We are not ready to report on that' or 'We have never decided to do such a thing' or, 'We will have a full report on that at a later date,' or even, 'We can't comment on that.' The point is, we will not always tell everything we know, and we will not fabricate. The same thing is true if we need to deal with a threat. We will not use the phrase, 'If you do, we will respond with... whatever.' I do not think government should ever make a definite threat unless it is willing to follow through with it, and I don't believe in making the threat specific. We will always defend ourselves, but I am not about to reveal the method. Now, in all of this Ronald will keep you informed as to the definitive issues.

"As to the second kind of issues, again, the truth must prevail. If we all do our jobs honestly and diligently, we will never have to fear telling the truth. Just answer the questions as briefly as possible. It will speed up the news conference and help keep you out of trouble with other questions gleaned or implied in a lengthy answer.

"Also, don't be afraid to tell reporters that you don't know, if that is true. Then add, if possible, that you will try to find the answer for the next press conference."

At that point a few others in the group felt more comfortable, enough so that they asked Ward and Ronald about items pertinent to what was just summarized because that issue was pertinent to the tenor of the entire administration. Ward permitted it to continue for a few minutes and then asked another person—one who had remained quiet to that point—if he had any questions. He did, and so did others. This continued for nearly an hour. Then Ward stood. "Our time for today is over. We will periodically do this again. I thank you for your willingness to talk freely. That's what I want. Now we all have our own work and we need to get to it."

Because the two-party system had been almost eliminated during the change toward the new national election process, the new Congress had been "organized" along different lines. Naturally, there were people who were in various groups; ranging from the far "right" to the far "left" and everywhere in between. However, certain individuals were more naturally gaining in popularity and respect. Both of those personal qualities were enhanced when the president invited such a representative group to meet with him that morning.

Ward continued his opening "welcome" in the same style he always used, emphasizing openness, honesty, and discussion. Again, this meeting lasted for one-and-one-half hours, with a congenial departure for all.

Leaving the White House, these "leaders" of Congress expressed to each other their pleasure with this start of a relationship between executive and legislative powers. Their hopefulness would show itself in further cooperation among their colleagues in Congress. Everything seemed to be "coming up roses" for the nation. Time would tell.

The Cabinet spent the first half hour of its next meeting updating the president on its progress of moving toward proposals regarding suggested ideas. Work on that would continue. Members also reported on some staff changes, along with their meetings with leaders of the separate government departments.

For the last half hour, Wards offered more ideas for the members to consider. "I want your thoughts for and against such things as: eliminating unrelated amendments to all bills voted by Congress; conducting a definitive study of church/state relationship as mentioned in the Constitution; a study on the implications therein regarding 'the right to bear arms,' especially as it relates to 'in order that' an army would be available; how the 'separation of powers' relates to presidential pardons and presidential nomination of Supreme Court Justices.

"We should also start discussing how to progress further in ecological improvements, closing tax loopholes, advancing clearer 'Truth in Advertising,' improvements in our national educational system, and clarifying and lessening government subsidies of all kinds. Again, I stress that we are only in the thinking process in all of this. So, make certain you limit the number of persons involved at this point. We will become more definite and specific when we decide what and how and 'if' we are going to proceed."

Dianne, the Secretary of Defense, broke the brief silence that followed. "Remembering your ideas concerning peace and prosperity, I have been working on ideas to reduce the cost of our armed forces without lessening our defense ability. In fact, with some recent technology, I will soon be able to give specific suggestions to this Cabinet so we can discuss them, decide, and move forward. Of course, I do have a few people researching causes of war in history, along with suggestions for lessening and eliminating those. It has been going very well and I am pleased with my staff's enthusiasm and ability."

Ward gave a few positive nods and thanked Dianne. "I welcome any other updates." One after another, each member gave brief comments. All were positive in nature, so the president felt the need to end the meeting with these words, "I hope you all understand we are yet in the 'honeymoon' period of our administration. The time will come quite soon when that is over—especially when we make definite proposals to Congress. Don't worry about that. Just keep doing honest and diligent work and the rest will take care of itself.

"Thank you all for your work and your participation. I'll see all of you at the next meeting, if not sooner. God be with you."

Chapter 5:
"Caution Ahead"

Ward walked back to the Oval Office with his Chief of Staff, asking, "How do you see things, Ronald?"

"As you stated, Mr. President, it is yet the 'honeymoon' time, and we are just in the thinking stage of our work. But, I am pleased with what has been going on so far. I am also more convinced that you were the right choice for this job. Thanks again for agreeing to run."

"It all seems like a dream to me. But I must say that I like it. I hope it is not a 'power' thing for me, but, rather, that I'm happy to be in a position that allows me to work toward what I believe is God's call to this nation. That was not possible for a parish pastor. Now we have a chance, at least. The rest I leave in God's hands."

"'Pray as though everything depends upon God and work as though everything depends upon you.' Isn't that one of your favorite quotes?"

"One of them," was Ward's answer, pleased that Ronald had remembered.

At the Oval Office, the two of them did some review, but mainly dealt with future schedules and agenda. One of the projections had to do with a Roosevelt "fireside chats" style of brief, monthly reports on radio and television. Weekly "chats" would take place on the President's website, which remained very popular. It was also the source of many suggestions which staff members organized and condensed into a daily report for Ronald.

While the presidential "honeymoon" lasted for a few months, Ward was awakened very early by the telephone on what would probably have been an otherwise beautiful spring day. "Yes," he said, trying not to disturb Lisa. After listening for a few seconds he softly responded, "I'll be right there."

The Defense Secretary and the Chief of Staff of the Armed Forces were waiting, along with Ronald. All went into the Oval Office. "What are the details?" the president asked as he closed the door.

"So far the call has not been traced to a specific source, but we will know within a few minutes. The threat was vague. Specifics are to be delivered soon, but we are taking it very seriously. Whoever it is there is already enough information to assure us that we are dealing with someone of great intelligence and skill. Our military profiler has us convinced that we can't toss this aside as some foolish trick. The next call will be patched through to your phone here. That was the first specific demand of the caller. The others will be detailed when he calls again. We would not be bothering you with this yet, except we are convinced it is too serious to ignore."

"Thank you. I'm glad you did. When are we to receive the next call?"

"In about half an hour: exactly at 3:00 am."

The four of them talked about possible responses, but the vagueness of the first communication made that difficult. The caller had given enough "secret" information to make a convincing argument to speak with the president, but that was all. Apparently he wanted an immediate response from the president without a chance for any thought ahead of time.

At 3:00 am, the president's telephone rang.

Chapter 6:
"Work As Though
Everything Depends Upon You"

"This is President Adamson speaking." Ward then paused to listen. He had answered the phone with the speaker on so the others could hear. He also knew that everything was being recorded and traced, so he had been asked to keep the caller on the line as long as possible.

The Secretary of Defense had assured the president that new technology had begun and was continuing that work of tracing since the first call had been received. She was on another line with her own office, awaiting some definite information regarding the location of the caller. Several teams of intercept groups had been stationed around general areas believed to be somewhat near the source of the first call. When that location became definite, a decision needed to be made by the president to either order a forced intercept or not. Ward would make that decision based upon what he heard from the caller and also the group assembled in his office.

The voice was distorted, yet easily understood. "I will be brief. I know this call is being traced, but you won't succeed. I want one billion dollars wired to an account address I will send you. If you refuse, about one million U.S. citizens will die. You have until this time tomorrow to agree."

"Wait a minute," Ward quickly interjected. "How do I know this threat is real?"

The caller answered quickly, before Ward could say anything else. "I have already given validation of that fact to your defense department. If they had not believed me, you would not be on the phone now."

Ward quickly spoke again, "I will need to talk further with them before I decide. And I also need time to acquire the money to be sent."

"You have until this time tomorrow!" Then the line went silent.

"We have a location," was the quick response of the Secretary Yang. "Our nearest intercept group is already on the way. They will not deploy directly without your word. They will remain invisible observers until that time."

The first question from Ward came quickly. "Do you have any idea concerning his threat of murdering a million people?"

"We are working on that also, now that we know his location. If it is some nuclear device, we have sensors to detect it. If he has arranged some way to set it off by remote control, we also have the ability to prevent the signal from leaving his presence. My guess is that the device would be some distance from him, so that he could call again and demand more money the next time. I assure you that—as smart as he is—we have even greater intelligence and technology."

"But, are we taking a chance?" Ward questioned again.

"Everything is a chance," Dianne Yang responded, "but we have run trial games similar to this situation and are as well prepared as possible. I strongly believe we can take this person without any problem."

Ward thought about it for a few second and then asked, "What do the rest of you think I should do?"

The Secretary of Homeland Security, Jacob Smith; Chief of Staff, Ronald Albright; General Mark Brighton; and Vice President Robert James agreed that this administration should not give in to any terrorist. General Brighton added, "It is also possible that this guy is faking. I think it boils down to which of us has the best technology. I have worked with enough companies and government agencies to believe that we have the upper hand in this."

"I also agree with that," Bob agreed. "The same has been my experience in business dealings."

The discussion continued for a little while, thinking of possible scenarios. Then the Defense Secretary's phone buzzed once more. "Yes, Major. Secretary Yang here." She listened for about thirty seconds. "Just a minute." She muted the phone and looked at the president. "Sir, the intercept group has the location under surveillance and has run some tests, some of which I already told you about. We are now convinced it is not only a hoax. They await your order to neutralize the situation and apprehend this person. But, they will saturate the air waves just in case he has some remote device to denote a distant bomb. It is your decision."

The president sat quietly in prayer for a few moments. He looked up and ordered, "I'm convinced. Do it!" Ward breathed deeply and bowed his head again as Secretary Yang gave the order over the phone.

There was silence for a long time. No one wanted to say anything else. It was as if they were listening and waiting for some atomic bomb to explode.

The atmosphere in the Oval Office was heavy with their nervousness. Then the lights in the office and the area outside, for as far as they could see, blinked and dimmed for several minutes. Secretary Yang broke the silence, "Don't worry. That is just the result of the power that is preventing any remote from carrying a signal. It means that our group is entering its objective. It should be over in a few minutes."

No one answered. In a few minutes, the lights steadied again and the phone rang. "Yes," was all that Ward said when he answered it.

The phone was on the speaker still, and a voice boomed into the room. "Mr. President, Sir, I am pleased to report the complete success of our mission. We have the man in custody. When we entered he did push a button on a remote, but our saturation device worked perfectly. Nothing else happened. I await further orders."

It was a nervous response from the president. "Thank you." Some tears formed in his eyes. "I want to meet you here this morning and thank you and your men personally. I'll let General Brighton give you any further orders."

The head of the joint chiefs took the phone. "Secure the area. Leave a guard until we get a group of investigators there. I want to know the details of this guy's technology. Then report to my office in the Pentagon."

"Yes, Sir."

"And, thank you."

"You're welcome, Sir."

The atmosphere in the room was much lighter now. All shook hands and gave brief, nervous laughs as they left the office. Ward and Ronald hesitated and looked at each other. "Good work, Mr. President. I learned a long time ago to trust the judgment of an ESTJ personality when you have all the information."

"I hope I won't have to make another one like this."

Ronald smiled and replied, "When we find out the details, maybe we can use this incident to prevent others like it. Remember, we are on record that we will not make a deal with terrorists. This should prove it to everyone. I am very proud of you. The past months have really been worth the effort. You definitely proved that this morning. Good night, Mr. President. Or, I guess I need to rephrase that. Good day!"

Ronald and the rest left, and Ward made his way to the residence, hoping that Lisa had remained asleep through all of this. He wondered about how much he could tell her. Well, that could wait until he got a couple more hours of sleep.

The President of the United States had difficulty going right to sleep. He was tired, but his mind replayed the events of the early morning and was filled with both anxiety about what could have happened and thanksgiving to God that it did not. Eventually he had dozed off until he awoke later than his usual time. Lisa was no longer in bed. The first thing he did was to call and cancel his morning walk. He then found Lisa in the other room. "Good morning," they each said and then kissed with a hug. Ward hugged her closer than usual.

"Well," she responded, "aren't you the amorous one so early in the day!"

He released his hug and looked into her face. "It was a long night. I had a very early call and then a meeting in the office. We had a terrorist/blackmailer event. It could have been very bad, but turned out alright. I want to tell you a little about it before we have breakfast." They sat down, but he continued to hold her hand as he briefly recounted the events. "I did not want to wake you, even when I got back to bed, and then it took me a while to get to sleep. I canceled my walk for this morning because I didn't sleep very much when I got back. Are there any questions? I told you most of it. The rest we will know after the investigation is over."

"I don't think I need to know anything else. I'm just so thankful it turned out the way it did. It is difficult to imagine a million people vanishing in an instant. Might we pray now instead of at breakfast? I would think that others would not need to know the cause of our thanksgiving."

"I think that would be best." They prayed and tears of gratitude for safety came before they were done. They showered, dressed, and then ate the first meal of the day without very much conversation. Then, each went to their respective offices as Ward told Lisa, "We'll talk more after lunch."

The rest of the morning was filled for the president, but he was able to delay a few appointments for early afternoon. Both he and Lisa needed some off time to digest information about the threat. Ward did receive updates about it, but needed some time to consider how it would finally be reported to the nation—as well as its use to prevent any consideration of it being repeated by others. He had already assured himself that it had been the correct decision on his part. He had thought for a long time that a hard line against such threats was the only way to proceed. Without that assurance that threats would not accomplish their intent, there would—assuredly—be other threats. He once tossed around in his mind the idea that if all nations agreed they would not allow a high-jacked airplane to land in their country, high-jacking airplanes would surely end.

The president did meet the major who led the force ending the threat. He was most profuse in his gratitude and recommended him for a military or congressional honor. He would let the major know later. The update about the event itself was quite thorough. A great deal of progress had been made during those early morning hours. The accused broke down and confessed all, even where the nuclear instrument had been placed. It was found and removed safely, although—if exploded—would have killed over a million people, as well as huge destruction and fallout. The man had not been a bad person at first, simply one who had suffered at the hands of unscrupulous superiors. Ward would order an investigation of them, even though the man would face charges on what he did.

The press had been given minimal information on the events, with the stipulation that it was an ongoing investigation. More information would be given later. That was, again, according to Ward's style. He first needed to discuss with those involved, and how best to use what had happened in order to stop this kind of human response to their own mistreatment. He had always believed that prevention was better than retribution; intervention better than punishment. At a meeting, years ago, the psychologist leading the group talked about mental illness, saying, "We put people away without trying to find out

'What did our society do to them to cause them such reaction? To what in our society were they so sensitive?'" That got Ward to thinking of better ways to deal with society's problems. As president, he now had a chance to make a difference.

Chapter 7:
"Pray As Though Everything Depends Upon God"

Ward always tried to teach people that his family worshipped every week, not because he was a pastor, but because he was a Christian. Everyone needed to thank and praise God frequently, as well as being open to the strength that God freely wants to give people.

That had not changed since he came to the capitol. At the beginning, the First Family started visiting some of the larger churches in Washington, especially the National Cathedral, which was the closest to his own Lutheran denomination. They also visited two Roman Catholic churches, as well as other Christian congregations. When he became president, they started to visit Lutheran churches in order to transfer their membership. After all, they would be there for six years. Further, they did not know where they would be following that term. Ward had worked hard for over thirty years to keep membership rolls up-to-date, and it was time for him to follow suit. They picked the one the closest to the White House and made arrangements for the transfer.

It was natural then for Ward and Lisa—and a number of Secret Service personnel—to be at worship the first Sunday following the bombing threat. Both Ward and Lisa were more somber and thankful for what they believed had been God's intervention in ending the bomb threat. The pastor used part of that event in his sermon and gave thanks to God for giving the president the knowledge and the courage and the faith to make the right decision.

When the service was over, there was a change in the usual dismissal pattern. Ward decided—against Secret Service advice—to remain during the fellowship time and greet the people present. Such a change did present a great deal of anxiousness among his security people, but Ward decided it was worth the risk—especially so because it had not been a pre-planned event. Both Ward and Lisa needed that personal touch, even though it would not become a pattern for the future. Following the end of the threat, they both felt the need for this extra time among fellow Christians. Christian faith stresses the importance of such community under God.

Chapter 8:
"The First Lady"

L isa had planned to spend the early morning working with her secretary, as well as with a few friends she had recruited to volunteer for a yet to be decided national "First Lady's Leadership Renewal." The general idea was to encourage a rebirth in volunteerism, first among women and later among men and young people. Lisa agreed with her husband that freely "acting in love toward neighbors" will not earn anyone eternal life, but it will bring more health and happiness to both the giver and the recipient in this life.

She had decided to have the meeting in the living room of the residential suite. That would be more comfortable and a great deal more informal than in any of the west wing conference rooms. Lisa was yet a little nervous about her role as "First Lady." She tried, in many ways, to lessen the distance between the first family and the rest of the people. Of course, she understood the great meaning of the presidency—and her role as First Lady—but her personality remained somewhat uncomfortable with that kind of "aloofness." Her secretary, Olivia Martin, interrupted her thoughts about all of that. "Everyone you invited has arrived, Mrs. Adamson."

"Thank you, Olivia. Let's go and get started." The two of them walked together and entered the first family's living room.

"Good morning, Mrs. Adamson," was the greeting from those present in the room when Lisa entered. Others quickly expressed their pleasure in being asked to help and included their eagerness to begin. Lisa smiled at those present and told them to sit again.

"Good morning to all of you, and thank you for accepting my invitation. I hope we will be able to accomplish a great deal in the years ahead. If we do, we should have a good foundation for the future work." That greeting was followed with Lisa walking around to each woman, greeting them with their names, and shaking their hands. She was amazed she was able to do that, but she had practiced and she had prayed for help to be able to do the complete greeting without forgetting any names or confusing them.

"My husband and I have known for many years that a paycheck is no guarantee that a person will actually do what is expected of them. In church work, most of the accomplishments were the result of unpaid volunteers. We have also noticed that such people were healthier and happier than the general population. We both know that God created all of us to be useful. There is strong evidence that when people no longer seem to be useful to others, they often become sick. Sometimes it happens that such a person might even die. It seems God has created us to have a purpose in this life. That is a lesson we will try to teach everyone in this nation.

"Olivia, my secretary, has prepared a summary of our previous ideas and planning. This will be the start of a file for each of you. Please add to it any ideas and suggestions that you can. We will then discuss them at our meetings and make joint decisions on all projects we undertake. Now, I want to listen to your thoughts about why we are all here."

During the next ninety minutes the room became alive with the combined enthusiasm of the women. They had ideas about helping government programs such as Medicare, Social Security, Education, Environment, National Parks, and others. The general thought was that volunteers could be used to monitor the operations of many programs: to make certain that funds given were used as prescribed. It had been known for many years that one of the biggest costs of government was the graft and misuse of funds with little oversight of the allotted money. Most government programs had a way of overspending and underachieving.

She recalled a government "Safe Streets" program in Indianapolis that was a prime example. The U.S. government had allocated a certain amount of money for the city to begin that program. The problem that ensued was this. After securing office space, a director, an assistant, secretarial help, and office equipment, the total amount of allocated money was gone. Nothing was left for the people it was meant to help.

So, Lisa was excited about that last suggestion to have volunteers who could be monitors for some government programs. "That would be an outstanding contribution," she added. "With all the information available electronically to us, all that is needed is people who can cross reference it so that a tremendous amount of money can be saved and put to a better use."

During their break, Lisa spent the time again acting as a hostess and getting to learn more about the lives of those with whom she would be working at least during the coming year. It was something she greatly enjoyed, as she had always been outgoing and friendly—a very real "people person." Her smile was never forced, always a natural result of her interest in people.

The rest of the morning was then spent in things more specific—getting organized and assigning responsibilities regarding research of issues. At the end, Lisa again thanked everyone. She also encouraged them in their work, emphasizing the good for the nation that they could accomplish.

Following that meeting, Lisa was able to have lunch with Ward. She talked with him about what had transpired at her meeting, especially commenting about the enthusiasm of those present. Ward listened carefully, simply expressing approving words from time to time. He did not want to comment further about Lisa's leadership or what had transpired because this was the First Lady's project. He knew Lisa well enough to trust that she would do an excellent job.

After finishing lunch, Ward returned to his own work and Lisa remained in the residence during the afternoon, inviting her secretary there for some friendly conversation, as well as long-range planning of her activities and "First Lady" appearances and responsibilities.

Chapter 9:
"Reading, Writing, 'Rithmatic"

Education Secretary Betty O'Donell was ushered into the Oval Office. Ward quickly rose from his desk and greeted her warmly. "Thank you for coming with such a short notice, Betty. I had a cancellation on my calendar and hoped you could be available."

"No problem, Mr. President. I DO work at your pleasure."

"Well, I hope you have pleasure in your work. Please sit down."

Ward began by outlining one of his concerns about educational flaws. "I remember George Bernard Shaw's comment that: 'The United States of America and England are the only two nations separated by a common language.' We have already talked a little about that. I would like to help change that perception. Have you thought about any possibilities?"

The secretary opened her brief case and removed two folders. "Sir, here is a copy of my thoughts on the subject." She handed one folder to the president, and then continued. "As you pointed out, the decline started gradually, but then increased in speed as the years passed. I believe that one of the big errors was when we stopped teaching Latin in our schools. I know it is a 'dead language,' but about sixty percent of our vocabulary is based on Latin. Not only that, but there is also the fact that we have lost most of the emphasis on the proper cases of nouns and pronouns and other parts of speech. We see it most often in the popular—yet, incorrect—use of 'I' and 'me.' In fact, it seems that the most common misuse is this: 'If you are like me, then....' It should be the nominative case 'I' rather than the objective case 'me.' The complete use would be, 'If you are like I am...' That was the illustration mentioned by you when we talked earlier. Of course, there are many other examples. There are also times when people speak using the word 'I' when the proper case is 'me'.

"Another example of confusing speech misusing 'I' and 'me' are these two sentences, which I have included in the report. They are: 'God loves you as much as me' and 'God loves you as much as I.' The first example means that God loves you and me to the same degree. The second example means both God and I love you equally."

Ward thanked her for remembering and agreeing with what had been mentioned during their first meeting. "There are many people who would claim this is just nit-picking, but I would argue otherwise. If we lose the ability to communicate accurately, we will have more serious problems. The best example of that possibility could be seen early in this century. Young people began 'texting' with a short-hand only they understood. In fact, many began talking in that same manner. If it continues, we will end up to be a people who will not be able to talk to each other succinctly and clearly. That could be a huge problem."

Betty had been nodding in agreement as the president had been speaking. Then she continued. "There is also the need to review the use of punctuation marks in our written communications. For example, look at these written statements. We have the same words in both sentences, but different meanings because of the punctuation." She handed the president a paper on which was written, "Mr. Brown said Miss Green is a very good teacher." "Without any punctuation, it means the good teacher is Miss Green. The same would be true if you put quotes before 'Miss' and after 'teacher.' But, if you enclose Mr. Brown with quotations marks and a comma, and also a comma and quotation marks before 'is' and quotation marks after 'teacher,' it is Mr. Brown who is the good teacher. I show that on the next page."

Ward turned the page, and there it was written as she had said: "Mr. Brown," said Miss Green, "is a good teacher."

"I believe we need to work on an educational program requiring that a foreign language be necessary for high school graduation. I think the situation has developed to that kind of seriousness. I would prefer that there would be at least one year of Latin, but it could be any present-day language. Not only would it improve our population's English, but it would also benefit our peoples' lives in this multi-cultured world—especially if students take two or more years of any language."

Ward quickly scanned the rest of her report and then began their discussion. They spent the next hour doing so and then concluded their meeting. "I appreciate what you have done. This is much more than I thought you would accomplish in such a short time. I will look it over more completely, and we will meet quickly before our next staff meeting and make any changes we want before we present it to the Cabinet as a proposal for their consideration."

The education secretary left, and Ward went to his desk to prepare for his next appointment.

Chapter 10:
"From the Website"

W ard began quickly when he entered the room. The full Cabinet had arrived just before he did. "You will notice in your agendas that I have listed some items I would like studied. A few are ideas I have had for many years, and all are suggestions gleaned from our website. We'll go quickly down the list. I want each of you to specifically note those related to your departments. However, I welcome ideas related to all departments from anyone.

"First on the page is a suggestion that we stop mowing along our national highways. A great deal of money is spent in that work—time, equipment, fuel, repairs, and pollution. But, in addition, such 'beautification' has also destroyed many beneficial plants, with a trickle-down effect involving many birds. I do not think that allowing such plants to grow presents any danger to the motoring public. In fact, I think those wild plants and flowers give us a more beautiful landscape than the mowing does. We need a study to find a better and less expensive way of meeting the needs of our highway system. If we begin such a program with our interstate system, perhaps the states will catch on to the premise that the present 'beautification' mowing is neither beautiful nor economical or good ecology."

The Transportation Secretary, Lyle Evers, spoke during the pause. "My office has also received suggestions relating to that. Of course, there were also objections to it, mainly because it would put a lot of people out of work—both in terms of the mower drivers and also those who build and maintain the machines. I have already assigned someone to get us facts about the items involved."

"Thank you, Lyle. I always appreciate that kind of responsible anticipation. Does anyone else care to comment? No? Okay. Then, let's move on to the next.

"TV ads from lawyers have advertised for a long time that they can help people eliminate or lessen the amount of money people owe for taxes."

The Secretary of the Treasury, Helen Baker, was nodding her head and quickly spoke. "I have looked at a report about that, and, like Lyle, I am having a study made of it. We are also preparing a procedure to stem the tide in these situations. It is a part of a review of our entire tax structure. For too many years there have been a large number of people and corporations who have been able to evade federal taxes either by creative bookkeeping or by simply not paying. There are also those who locate fake headquarters in other nations to avoid our taxes. That is not fair to those who pay what they should. The report should be in a workable form for our discussion in a month from now."

"Helen, my thanks go to you, also, for that foresight. You all make me look better as an administrator than I really am. But, I learned many years ago that the secret to being a good administrator is to surround oneself with competent people. I seemed to have picked the right people. Thank you."

Ward continued with the suggestion list. There were some concerning TV: programs needed to begin and end exactly on time; there should be no more printed words in TV commercials than can be read completely in the time they remain visible; commercials must be truthful in all respects, and there needs to be restriction on the number/time for commercials during each half hour. Regarding the Legal System: our court trials need to be quicker, without sacrificing the validity of any judgment. Suggestions were given that "a jury of one's peers" should be just that, and not one selected by the lawyers. Larger law firms had developed a system by which they could discern which "peers" would give a judgment in their favor and which would not. Also, there need not be that time before and at the end of a trial when lawyers tell the jury what they are going to present and then tell them again what they have shown—let the trial be one of facts and truth and then let the jury decide. It was also included that the judge should make a decision based upon law and not be influenced by family comments. Such comments about the individual on trial are completely outside of the law.

It was those kinds of public issues which were on the minds of the people. It was to such improvement in society that Ward had pledged himself to diligently work during his six-year term. It was in regard to such a task that the members of the Cabinet had been chosen by Ward. When the meeting adjourned, Ward knew all of his preliminary work had been worth the effort.

Chapter 11:
"Time Flies in Good Times"

The first year passed quickly for both Ward and Lisa. She had kept busy as the First Lady—a majority of the time having been spent leading her projects and encouraging volunteerism aimed at improving the quality of life for all citizens. Because of her efforts—and the multitude of volunteers she had recruited—the nation witnessed pleasant changes in education, national parks, health care, and various other areas of life in the United States of America.

Personally, her love and appreciation of her husband deepened as she experienced the increase in his love and trust in her. Busy as they were in their public lives, they both possessed the same values.

She often told Ward she was glad for the past year, even though she had silently been skeptical when the idea had first been presented that Ward run for president. Her work as a nurse during her marriage to Ward had been suspended while in the White House, but Lisa's self-esteem grew even more because of her work and success as First Lady. "It really feels wonderful to have been able to accomplish all those things" was a constant response to frequent compliments concerning her work.

Lisa and Ward both hoped that her programs of volunteerism would continue after they were gone. It was to such a goal that she continued with her plans and worked.

Chapter 12:
"Looking Back"

While the new system of national government had changed to such a degree that many problems were able to be solved more quickly, there—naturally—remained many differences of opinions. There was nothing the administration could do to eliminate such things among the voters, but the people involved with governing had learned how to disagree without being disagreeable. They also had grown to a maturity which debated the issues, then voted, and then moved on. Among all of the lawmakers and administrators a general understanding of: "you do your best, and you win some and you lose some, and then it is over."

Ward had his last Cabinet meeting of the year. Most of it involved talking about what had been accomplished, as well as seeking ways to strengthen the procedures which would ensure continuance of the goals they had set.

"Our first order of the day is a very personal one for me," Ward began. "I have come to greatly appreciate Bob as my vice president. I have learned much from him, and I am pleased he is a part of this administration."

"I appreciate your support, Mr. President. I also have appreciated how you are governing this nation. Thank you for your leadership. Thank you for including me in many decisions. I look forward to the next five years."

After a few minutes of similar remarks from others, the conversation turned to finalizing reports for each department. It was noted that, although there was room for more improvement, a great deal had been accomplished. They were all eager to start the second year. All agreed it had been worth the effort.

BOOK FIVE

Chapter 1:
"From the Top Again"

With the passing of the first year it was time for the annual State of the Union address to Congress. The formalities of the invitation and the scheduling from Congress to the president took place in January, and all were gathered for the joint session. The president was announced and everyone stood as Ward entered to the applause, which was much more sincere and energetic than it had been for previous "party" administrations. It was a new day. It was a much better day. The new way of having elected a president had proven itself in the previous twelve months.

When all the waving, handshakes, greetings, and formalities had taken place, Ward again looked over the assembly and began his formal speech. "I hope most of that applause was for you, rather than for me. Presidents are never the main work behind government. As I have often said, and as you all know, the leadership work of this nation is done by Congress. As each of you represent the people and the nation to which you are held responsible, true democracy works.

"It has worked very well this past year. You have all done the work for which you were elected. If the politicians of the past had done what you have accomplished, there would not have been a need to change the political process. You have proven that the present, better way has been worth the effort of making that change. The nation thanks you. I thank you. We have gotten much closer to fulfilling the dream of our founding fathers.

"The state of the nation has improved significantly during the past twelve months. That was possible only because of the awakening of the voters' responsibility. Starting with an historic ninety-two percent of eligible voters, it is now true that this is a government BY the people. It is also true—based upon the social changes that you (Congress) have made—that we now also have a government FOR the people. Together, that makes this a time in which we truly have a government OF the people.

"Specifically, world-wide agreements have greatly reduced the possibility of costly wars. Those agreements have joined with new technology to completely isolate any group or nation thinking to destroy world peace. We and all peaceful peoples are safer now than at any time during history. That safety has given us savings of finances, human life, and resources, which all nations can put to better use for the sake of both people and the earth itself.

"A particular benefit of such savings is the giant leap forward in medical research. A part of the money that used to be channeled to kill people is now producing ways to bring better health to all humans. We know no one will live on earth forever, but while you remain residents of this earth, you ought to be able to live life with joy rather than with pain.

"One of the greatest problems of national government is the ability to manage. The greater the number of people for which any government is responsible, the more difficult it is. That fact has caused many problems for this nation in the past. I believe we have made great progress in solving that. Our method is the use of volunteers who will keep all of us informed in areas where national government simply doesn't have the number of people necessary to know what is happening throughout the entire country.

"The 'boss' of the first family has worked hard to help us with a solution. Believing that God has created all of us to be useful, and knowing that nothing good happens to us when we are not useful, my wife has started to develop a huge core of volunteers. They are eager to increase the truth that we are and need to be a government OF, FOR, and BY the people. This administration will also continue the use of my website for that purpose. This government will no longer be aloof, untrustworthy, and inaccessible to the people of this land."

While there had been applause at various times during his speech, there was very loud applause at this point—even a standing ovation. The president had hit a sensitive nerve of the nation. For too long, politicians had become "removed" from the general public—at least until they campaigned for re-election. And, even then, the crowds to which they spoke had been mainly by invitation only.

When it quieted again and everyone sat down, Ward continued. "I see this nation moving to the forefront of what I have always believed to be God's Call—God's Purpose—for these United States of America. I am certain we were called into existence to be the power behind bringing world peace to this planet. But, I also believe God's Call was meant for us to focus on two objectives.

"The first goal was to bring about peace between all peoples and all governments of this globe. We have almost achieved that. God has led us to the edge of such total freedom from war. I feel very confident that in the next year or two we will have succeeded.

"The second goal is to bring ecological peace to the lands, air, and waters of this creation. We have begun that work, yet much more remains before us.

We have slowed the causes of pollution of the earth, and will soon begin the process of renewal. That is very good news for all of creation. That is great news for the future of this earth."

There was another round of applause following those words. Everyone had been aware of the better situation regarding ecology, but it was good to hear the official announcement. Then the president continued. "Those two goals have been interrelated. Much of it has to do with the absence of the expense of war. Good ecology of people and earth costs a great deal. But, money and resources not used for wars has now been put to better use for people and planet.

"I do need to mention my gratitude to those responsible for this nation's advances during the past twelve months. I begin by telling you of an experience in my past life as a pastor of a large congregation. In one of my conversations years ago with a businessman with a great deal of common sense, he told me this. He said, 'When I get to heaven, I want to see my grandfather and tell him I am thankful for what he had done for me. He had started my business and passed it on to me through my father. I want to be able to tell him: "Thank you for all of that. I am happy to have taken what you gave me and continued to improve it."'

"We talked about that 'life-process'—that no one achieves on his own. Every one of us stands on the shoulders of those who came before us. The same is also true in government. If I have been successful this past year, it was possible only because I have stood and I remain standing on the shoulders of those who came before me. That continues even now. This administration has been successful because of the many people who support me. This administration has been successful also because of the support of the present Congress. This Congress has been successful because of the support of the voters and the people of this great nation, as well as all who have gone before us. All of you who hear my voice share in that community of success. I thank God for all of that history. I pray that we will be able to continue in that faithfulness with each other—and allow God to give us further success.

"I do not wish to extend this speech concerning those many items with which you are familiar. All of us will continue working in the coming year to correct what is yet in error, to strengthen what is right, and to continue to guarantee that the resources of this earth will be put to uses which bring joy and hope to all people.

"Thank you for your share in this great mission. I personally thank all of you with words so familiar to me: 'Well done, thou good and faithful stewards.'"

It was that kind of sharing of gratitude, common to Ward's style, that prompted a great applause and cheering from the entire rising Congress. Ward had turned from the podium, but he turned back to the assembly, waved his hand, and began to join in the applause. He knew it had been a joint effort between legislative and administrative members—both approved by an informed and active population of voters.

Chapter 2:
"We Are Not Alone"

As Ward began his second year as the leader of the United States of America, the president's office received a request from the president of France that the two of them meet to discuss and resolve a few mutual issues. When Chief of Staff Albright brought this request to Ward's attention, the president and he began a discussion about possible procedures for such a discussion.

Ward thought back to his college classes in political science. He told Albright, "I remember my professor explaining that he did not believe that heads of state should ever be directly involved in such discussions. When the top persons come to a decision, there is no way out of it. But, if at least two other people discuss issues and arrive at a consensus, then there is room 'at the top' for either or both presidents to reject or modify it without creating a national crisis."

The chief of staff thought about that for a short time and then responded, "That makes sense. However, how we do handle this personal request without creating an international incident?"

"I think I should handle that part of it myself," was Ward's answer. "I'll call him and invite him for a personal visit. I'll also explain my position and reasons, including that such a different process is to his advantage, too. He and I can simply have a pleasant visit, dinner, and so forth while others have the formal discussions. Later, when they are done, he and I can talk about the decisions privately ourselves, and then we both can see if those decisions should be made public without any changes."

"I guess that would take care of it in a better way and eliminate problems down the road." Albright was impressed with Ward's thinking. "After you have contacted him, and if he agrees, you will also need to ask about the nature of those 'mutual issues.' Then I can set up the meeting with the proper officials."

"I agree. I'll try to get him right now so that you can listen to what he has to say." Ward buzzed his secretary to give him the information. "Henry, try to get the president of France for me so I can talk with him about his request. This might be a convenient time for him." While Henry Jacob, his secretary, worked at getting the president of France on the phone, Ward and Ron began to talk about other items on their daily agenda.

In a short time, Ward's phone buzzed with the secretary's message that the president of France was on line two. Ward thanked him and greeted his French counterpart. After a short explanation by Ward and a couple of questions for him, the president of France agreed with Ward on the change. Ward then got a briefing concerning the mutual issues. A date for the meeting was agreed upon, and they told each other the number of persons who would be specifically involved with the discussions.

Because the mutual issues were energy and defense, Ward's chief of staff made a note to immediately contact Irwin Cook, Energy Secretary; Dianne Yang, Defense Secretary; and Milton Berry, Secretary of State. He would give them the details, and each would contact the other persons in their departments who would be invited to the discussions.

Ward and Ron then returned to their previous agenda and finished up that planning. "Is there anything else I can do for you, Mr. President?"

"No, Ron. I know you have things here under control, and I really appreciate your attention to detail. I'm glad you accepted the chance to stay on here."

"I serve at your pleasure, Mr. President." Then Ron left to do his job.

Chapter 3:
"Friendly Persuasion"

The French/United States "Conference" went well. Because of the way it was organized—and also due to the quality of the people involved—both Ward and the president of France spent only a short time discussing the "final" agreement. Both were pleased with the wording and the expected results. They also worked on a press release and agreed to a joint public report just prior to the state dinner that evening.

Each man thanked the other for what had taken place. They also agreed that such a method was a much better way of conducting international agreements. Although neither expected much fallout from their decisions, they both felt better that—in case it would be needed—they had a "way out" of said agreement because neither had been directly involved in the discussions and decisions.

That made the evening much more enjoyable. Following a very brief public report outside of the White House, the two presidents went into the state dinner. Once again, Lisa and the French First Lady filled the role of hosts. The last two persons they greeted were their husbands. All four of them then entered the banquet and were greeted with a standing ovation.

After the dinner there was entertainment by personalities from both nations. Then, at a reasonable hour, final toasts were made and people began to depart. Ward and Lisa were the last to leave the room, but not before offering their appreciation to the dinner staff, especially to the head chef. He had prepared an excellent combination of U.S./French cuisine, which had impressed people from both sides of the Atlantic.

In the residence, Ward and Lisa sat in a love seat and relaxed. They held hands and talked about the day, much of which Lisa had spent with the French First Lady while Ward had a pleasant, friendly time with her husband. It had been a very good day for them and for both of the nations involved. In addition, there would be advantages for most of the world. It was one of those kinds of decisions.

Later, in bed, Lisa curled up in Ward's arms and passionately kissed him. "Just think, I spent most of my day with the First Lady of France."

"Well, don't forget she spent most of her day with the First Lady of the United States." Both gently shook their heads in amazement of where they were and how their plans for their lives had changed so rapidly. "One never knows what any tomorrow will bring. We simply trust God and try to do what is right."

"That's what I have always done," was Lisa's response. "That's why I married you."

After another kiss, they turned out the light....

Chapter 4:
"Another Test Today"

I t was very early—about 3:00 am—when the president's bedside telephone buzzed: not a good sign. Ward grabbed the cordless and walked out of the bedroom as quietly as possible, closing the door behind him. "I have General Brighten on hold for you, Mr. President."

"Put him on."

"Mr. President," the head of the joint chiefs of staff began. "We have a situation that needs your attention. A rebel group in China has begun attacking government installations. Premier Sheng notified us, as our agreement stated. He has deployed his troops in a defensive mode, awaiting response from the World Council." Ward and General Brighton quickly discussed what world governments had planned in order to respond to similar situations.

It had taken several years for both technology and diplomacy to advance enough for such agreements to gain acceptance by all of the major powers in the world. But, eventually, the agreements had been made because of the danger and cost of continuing with numerous wars. Added to that was the knowledge that money spent on wars would find better use in keeping peace in the world. People of the world would live longer, healthier, and more prosperous lives.

When a situation would arise—similar to this problem in China—the power of the entire world would be used to end it and punish those foolish enough to break the peace. Naturally, the nation involved would first of all put into action its own containment plans. But the next step would be a world-wide response of the technology and force available to bring any uprising to a quick end—followed by a World Court appearance for those involved.

The peace had lasted for a few years. Those with any degree of power were convinced that no one would ever again benefit from war, and the peace that had been achieved was too valuable to change. Even then, though, the possibility always existed that someone would be foolish enough to "test" the system. The result was the phone calls going on around the world. The brief discussion between Ward and General Brighton was only one of many happening world-wide at the same time. Meanwhile, all available technology was already being used to contain the revolt and stop it immediately.

As soon as Ward gave the order to the general, the Joint Chief of Staff passed on the "go" to appropriate people at the pentagon. The same thing was happening in all World Council nations. Before the sun rose in Washington, Ward received another call from the pentagon. It was good news. "The uprising has been stopped. There have been no further deaths or damage." General Brighton was upbeat in his report. "All that remains is the systematic rounding up of the insurgents and their imprisonment to await trial."

"Thank you for your quick action, General. Although I hated to see someone test the resolve of the rest of the world, it is heartening to see that all the planning has done its job. I think it will be a long time before anyone else tries the same thing. Peace is always a lot better than war."

"Although I am trained to fight in war," the general responded in agreement, "I must admit that our present defense against war is a lot better way to live. It is also easier on the casualty list."

After a few other comments, the call ended and Ward returned to the bedroom. Lisa remained asleep and Ward simply sat in a chair, rather than disturb her. In a short time he fell asleep with a prayer of thanksgiving to God for the peaceful outcome of the morning's problem.

When Lisa woke, Ward went to their bed. "How is my Sleeping Beauty? Did you have a good night?"

"Actually, it was restful. I did have a dream that you had to get up early, but that was all."

"That may not have been a dream at all, Lisa. I did have to get up very early." He then told her what had happened.

"Wow! The World Council plans did work."

"They went exactly as they were planned. It is all over now except the final judgment by the World Court. Thank God for big favors!"

"And also for small favors."

Chapter 5:
"It Was Inevitable"

It was inevitable. It only took a month into the second year for it to happen. The Press Secretary, Jim Thomson, had gotten through his report and was about ten minutes into the questioning when he was asked, "Will you comment on the report that this administration is working on a vast overhaul of our educational system?"

It took Jim by surprise, but he quickly replied, "What report? What do you mean?"

The reporter stood and looked at his notes. "My paper was offered some specific information about proposed changes to educational programs in this nation—for a price. We are about to move further on this, but I decided to include any responses from the administration."

"I don't know about any, such report, so I will have to check on it and get back to you."

"What if we simply print what we have?"

The press secretary was very quick to respond again. "You are always at liberty to print whatever you want, but you ought to verify what you have or risk your integrity as a reliable news reporter. I will check on this and get back to you."

A few others chimed in with additional question, but the press secretary held his ground and was finally able to recognize another reporter who changed the subject. The session ended soon after that.

When Jim left the room, he was met by Chief of Staff Ronald Albright. "You handled that very well. We need to answer it soon. Right now, you and I will meet with the president and find out how he wants to proceed."

It took a few minutes for President Adamson to return to the Oval Office. "I have called Education Secretary, Betty O'Donell, and she will be here shortly. Let me state that I am not that much disturbed by the leak concerning our discussions. We need only tell the truth. We are simply listing areas in public education as one of many ideas we have received for improvement in this nation's educational system.

"What disturbs me most is the probability that one of our staff has seen fit to try to sell or give information that should be kept 'in house.' So, I think we need to trace this back to the source and deal with it." The three of them spent a few minutes talking about that policy.

Education Secretary O'Donell was ushered in while they were discussing it. After greeting her and explaining their conversation so far, Ward added, "Ronald agreed with me that we need to find out the name of that person and then decide what we do about it. Has that been put into motion?"

"Yes. As soon as I finished talking with you, Mr. President, I put my best and most trusted assistant on it right away. I told him to be discreet about it at this point, but I am confident that we will know the name of the staff person involved in a short time."

"Thanks, Betty. Next, we need to give our reporter a quick response to his question. If we do, maybe we can keep a lot of it out of the papers. What do you all suggest?"

"Well," Jim responded first, "Mr. President, I think you already said it a minute ago. We can give a general summary of the way this administration brainstorms ideas of possible improvements for the lives of people in this nation, especially the many ideas we receive through our website. In the case of education, we can honestly state—as I did in the press conference—that there is no report, that so far we have only a list from that 'brainstorming.' We could even publish the list as some of the ideas we will be thinking about. Some might be eliminated and others might be added. That is the way we work."

Ward nodded approval. "I knew I had picked you as press secretary for a reason. I like it. Actually, we won't be telling anything other than what has already been paid for by the paper and received. The only difference will be that none of those items have been discussed enough to be put into a report. Do it."

Jim was dismissed to write a response. He would bring it back to Ronald for final approval and then fax it to all of the reporters. The president, the chief of staff, and the education secretary remained in the Oval Office.

Betty spoke first. "This might turn out to be a blessing in disguise. It will let the voters know how we work and that we try to be honest with them, and that we will think about all kinds of options to make this nation even greater."

"That's why I was not too disturbed about this issue," was Ward's response. "The bigger problem is the sale of information that was to be only for our work."

At that moment, Ward's telephone buzzed. He had informed his secretary that he wanted to be interrupted by any call for the secretary of education. He answered, listened, and then said, "It's for you, Betty."

"Put it on speaker," the Education Secretary responded. Then she identified herself, "This is Secretary O'Donell. We have you on speaker in the Oval Office."

All heard the voice of Under-Secretary Harvey Green. "We got lucky, and we have the name you wanted."

"Good work, Harvey. The president and chief of staff are here. Tell us what you have."

"It wasn't too difficult. We found telephone records between the reporter and one of our staff. When we confronted him, he hesitated at first but finally admitted he made the contact. He also said he had asked for some payment but had not yet received anything. His name is Todd Browning, and he is employed in our records division. That is what we have now."

"Thank you, Harvey. Again, we appreciate the quick work. I should be back in my office soon, and I will handle it now."

"Well," the president remarked as he disconnected the call. "I'd like your comments on this issue." He looked to the chief of staff. "Ronald, you have been fairly quiet so far. What do you think?"

"I think this Todd needs to be fired. Government is not meant as an additional source of income for enterprising individuals. I also think that a memo (perhaps without mentioning his name or job) needs to be sent to all departments, underscoring the president's 'One Strike' policy. It probably was inevitable, and we are lucky it came with such a minor issue. However, we can't tolerate it or we will be hampered in our work."

With nodding agreement from all, the meeting adjourned, Secretary O'Donell returning to her office to dismiss an employee, most likely with a lecture regarding governmental ethics.

Chapter 6:
"Planning Ahead"

Although Ward knew that "the plans of mice and men oft go astray," he always had been a planner. That had been especially true in his sermon preparation, where he worked on sermons often three months in advance. He also followed to old traditions of spending one hour of preparation for every minute he preached. It was all related to his knowledge of planting ideas and then letting his brain do a lot of the work while he did other things.

While a lot of pastors delayed their sermon "writing" until Saturday evening, that had happened to Ward only once in his thirty-year ministry. It had been a very busy week with two funerals and two weddings, and he always spent a great deal of time on each. It was late Saturday afternoon before he was able to begin final preparation for Sunday, and it did not go well.

In addition to the anxiety of having so little time, his mind was also filled with things he had heard in the past, especially about a pastoral friend of his. That pastor had told him that he prepared his sermon in his mind as he walked up the steps to the pulpit. He had mentioned that to one of his own members after the worship service and the man simply replied, "After today's sermon, I think you need to add more steps to your pulpit."

Anyway, such a delay in preparation never happened again to Ward. He always took time to plan ahead. The same was true during his first year as president, and he began his second year with the same policy.

His chief of staff continually updated Ward with information gleaned from suggestions sent through the presidential website. Before the first Cabinet meeting, Ronald presented a copy of the best suggestions to date—those that had not yet been presented to the Cabinet for consideration. "Mr. President, here is a folder containing various ideas people have sent us through your website."

Ward took the folder and opened to the first page. He noticed several headings for various categories. He quickly glanced through then to get a general idea of the kinds of suggestions people had in mind. There were items related to television, professional sports, tax evaders, public schools, social security, and others. When he turned to the next page, he noticed each item contained more details about the suggestions, but also staff ideas about what could be done to implement them, which department of government should deal with them, and how the changes could be done under administration authority.

"My compliments go to you and your staff. I am also pleased we kept that website and that the people are serious about using it. I'll study this first and then we can plan some more on how to present it to the Cabinet." Ward checked his calendar for the next week and then continued. "I have enough time next Thursday for me to spend about two hours on it with you. Will 9:00 am fit your schedule?"

"Always," was Ronald Albright's quick response before they moved on to the usual early morning reports.

Of highest importance for Ward was to be well informed about as much of the gigantic federal government as possible. While he had to trust the people in his administration to do their jobs, and while it was impossible for him to keep up with every jot and title of what was taking place, Ward also agreed with President Truman's motto that "The Buck Stops Here."

For that reason, from time to time, Ward tried to spend time looking more closely at the workings, plans, and decisions of one department or agency at a time. It was impossible to be completely informed, but his method was better than nothing when heading up such an organization as a national government.

When Ward and his chief of staff met again, both were well prepared. The first item they discussed were various suggestions regarding television. A lot had changed during the history of TV. It was another example of "power corrupting practice." TV executives continued to push the limits of what was acceptable. Actually, they were like little children pushing the limits placed on them by parents to see how much their parents would permit. Ward had dealt with similar problems in his pastoral work.

Ward briefed Ronald on his own experience as a pastor. "When parents (or governments) do not enforce reasonable restraints, a certain progression happens. In the case of children, two responses could be expected. First, they would continue to push the limits even further. Secondly, something happened within their subconscious mind. Children basically look to their parents to determine what kind of person they might be when they grow to adulthood. Basically, children want to be strong. The problem with children who have 'weak and permissive' parents is that something happens within the subconscious of the child. Their parents are weak. They begin to worry they will probably grow up to be as weak as their parents. But, they do not want to be weak. That is a terrible condition for young people.

"I think it is also a terrible condition for governments, although most of the adults (who often act as children) don't really care about things like that. Most think only about the money and the power. But, the one thing that is exactly the same is that limits keep being pushed further and further away from what is normal and healthy for all concerned."

Ward and Ronald began their planning concerning television (as they would do with each suggestion), considering the federal government's right to regulate. As with all such things, the difference between state and federal rights was at the forefront. "Basically," Ronald began, "the central issue is always related to the boundaries of the states. Because television—similar to many other entities—crosses state lines, we have the constitutional authority to regulate what goes on. Sometimes people will stress 'freedom of speech' as the issue, but that is an extremely stretched argument."

"That would also be my argument, in addition to the fact that we do have the Federal Communication Commission," Ward continued that agreement with Ronald. "The first suggestion here has to do with the clock. I agree that the inconsistency of programs not starting and ending on time can be a problem for the viewers. Sometimes you miss the end and sometimes you miss the very beginning. Sometimes, programs are even scheduled to last one hour and five minutes, so that causes a problem if you want to watch something else on a different channel.

"I always believe that networks do it intentionally so you need to continue watching something on their own channel."

Ronald was nodding his head in agreement as he directed Ward's attention to suggested changes. "You will notice that suggestions have been given that would require all programs to start and end exactly on time, and that those time increments be exactly thirty minutes. That seems like a reasonable requirement. We have had the same suggestions from people who need to record programs for later viewing. They, also, run into problems with the present loose times."

"Okay. We will forward that to the FCC," was Ward's decision. "We need to suggest that the regulation allow for a five-second variance." Ronald agreed and wrote that down in his notes.

Ward continued: "The next item regarding television is one that has bothered me for years. There are all kinds of written 'disclaimers" in most of commercials. Some are so small, one can't even read any of it, and many are so long that they are not on the screen long enough to read more than a sentence or two."

Ronald was smiling as he continued that thought of Ward's. "Like you, I also think it is intentionally misleading by the advertiser. They give the good news in voice and then they want you to call them. It is only when they have you partly sold that they will somewhat 'spell out' the disclaimers that you were not able to read on your television screen."

"Yes," Ward added. "I think that is very deceitful. I also think that many people are sort of pushed into buying because of that method."

"The suggestion you have in your report is that we force the advertisers to change; that we require that anything written on the screen be big enough to read, and also kept on the screen long enough for the average person to read it entirely."

"I agree," Ward responded, "and we will also forward that to the FCC. What is next?"

Ronald looked at his report. "Well, this one is perennial in the minds of those who watch much TV. It has to do with commercials. People are convinced that they are getting out of hand and need to be regulated."

"I was under the impression that they were restricted to a certain amount of time per hour. But, it does seem there are many more than there used to be. In addition, most of the networks continue to interject all those advertising 'pop-ups.' Lisa has a fit about those."

"I have included in the report my own ideas, even though I don't know how many minutes of advertising per half hour would be acceptable. Somehow we need to have more monitoring of TV programs. But, that would require an army of people to do it successfully."

"I could ask Lisa for some help from her volunteer committee. If we get some directive from the FCC, Lisa might be able to get enough volunteers who would enjoy watching and timing such items."

"That could work. People could enjoy television at the same time they are serving their country." Ronald even seemed excited about the prospect of ending that problem in such a novel—and "cost-free"—method.

"Good," said Ward. "Why don't you have one of your staff check with the FCC about that idea?"

"I'll get on it right away, as soon as we finish."

Ronald's report contained other sections from the website which he and Ward talked about in less detail. Items such as sports at all age levels, tax problems, the complexity of government forms and reports, and transportation improvements were high on the list. Each would become the responsibility of a related Cabinet person. Their staffs would do the study and make suggestions for improvement. Meanwhile, Ward would check with Lisa about her volunteers' help with monitoring.

BOOK SIX

Chapter 1:
"Ladies' Turn"

"How was your day, Ward?" They were alone in the residence, and Lisa was hoping their evening would be free. She had not had a chance to talk much with her husband for the last week—just a short time at a few lunches. Of course, she had also been busy with a few of her own responsibilities, but her schedule was much shorter than the president's.

Ward gave her a loving kiss and hug before he answered. "I think it went quite well. It was a busy day, but I have never shrugged from my work. It helped that I have good people on my staff. How did things go for you? Did you miss me?"

"You know I did. But, you are home now—for the evening, I hope."

"As of now, the answer is 'yes,' but, I am the president. Anything could happen at any time."

"I am always aware of that, but I will take whatever time we have together. I do have a few things to talk about with you. Do I need an appointment? We have both been busy this past week."

"Well, do I need to make an appointment with the First Lady?"

"I am always at your call, Mr. President. Just don't get too used to it. Remember. You have a term limit as president—not a term limit as my husband."

"How could I ever forget that?" He hugged and kissed her again. "Are we ready for a nice leisurely dinner?"

"I called them the moment I knew you were on your way home. We should be eating in about fifteen minutes. I already have our cocktails on the table."

"Thank you. That would be great."

They went into the dining room and sat down—quite close to each other, as was their custom. Their first conversation was about their children. Lisa had been busy talking with the children on Skype. "I guess things are fine with all of them. Because it has been over a year since your big promotion, their notoriety has lessened and their lives are much more normal again, if that will ever be completely true from now on."

"Well, because of their ages and families, at least they don't have to live here with us. That makes it somewhat more normal for them." Lisa mentioned a few other details of their children's lives and then dinner arrived.

They ate at a normal pace, discussing current events, weather, future plans. When the table was cleared, they thanked the server and went into the living room, getting comfortable in one of the love seats—next to each other so that they could hold hands.

Lisa began the conversation. "I met this morning with the leaders of my women's group. They have been getting many more volunteers and assigning work. The only problem I see at this time is that we will run out of work to do in a short time, especially with a growing volunteer group."

"That's great," was Ward's response. "I don't only mean that things are going so well, but that more women are becoming interested in joining your group. That fits into something I want to discuss with you."

Lisa gave a slight smile, but she did not know what to think about Ward's words, particularly about what he wanted to discuss. "What is it?" was all she could ask.

"First of all, this is all in the planning stage. We don't even know if it will be possible—or legal—for us to do, but this is our thought. We have had suggestions about improving television viewing. One of our ideas is to set exact time limits for commercials. If that is possible, we need volunteers who would monitor commercials as they watch their own TV shows. I was thinking such a task would fit in with your volunteer group. Your women could assist in FCC monitoring of television at the same time that they enjoy watching."

"Is that all? That should be easy for us to do."

"Well, it is a little more involved, but it does not make sense to have laws when no one is checking to determine if they are being obeyed."

Lisa smiled at him. "I understand that. It is just the kind of thing we need in order for people to feel useful to their government. Should we discuss it at our next board meeting? We meet next Monday and do not have very much on our agenda. Of course, we won't make any decision until the Cabinet approves the idea, but we can develop a process for handling the monitoring."

"Of course. I will also put it on our next Cabinet agenda. You will keep me informed, won't you?"

"That depends on how nice you are to me."

"I'll try to keep that in mind."

At the board meeting, Lisa opened with a prayer—as was her custom—and asked for progress reports before presenting her husband's ideas. "I have a new idea for us directly from the president. This is very preliminary, and we do not want this idea to leave this room. It will be on the agenda for the next Cabinet meeting, but the president thought it best if it was presented to us first."

After she had given the basic idea, she asked for their thoughts. Three people tried to speak at the same time—there seemed to be great interest in the idea. Lisa smiled at their enthusiasm and then said, "Mary, why don't you speak first, then Betty, and then Amy?

Mary quickly spoke. "The president must have been reading my mind. I saw such suggestions on the website, and I was hoping that idea would make it to someone who could act on it. I am so happy we can have some part in making it happen." Betty and Amy briefly said the same, and then discussion proceeded.

No one disagreed with the concept because all had agreed with the reasoning for its need, and all were also pleased that they—as regular citizens—would have something to do about it. They were also honored with the possibility that they might have the responsibility of making certain it worked.

"My husband had hoped that you would be willing to be involved. There would be some extra, small items of management to determine. First of all, we would have to develop a schedule for the shows each person would monitor. But, I think we would have such a variety of likes and dislikes in viewing that it might not be any problem—probably not even any change."

Chapter 2:
"Moving Right Along"

W ard had Lisa's report in his hands as he opened the Cabinet meeting. "Before you in the folder is a new proposal which we will discuss for the first thirty minutes. The suggestions came from very many people using our website. I have discussed the legal issues with Steve Layton of Justice, also with the head of the Federal Communication Commission. Both of them assure me we are on solid ground with these ideas.

"You will note that I have included suggestions from my wife's women's volunteer group about how we could implement and monitor such a program— all without any additional staff or cost." Once the members had turned to the correct page, Ward continued. "The suggestion is that Lisa's group would make assignments to other volunteers who would be assigned certain networks and specific programs to watch and monitor. They would also record the program and send it to the FCC with a report if there are any extreme variations from whatever ruling is finally passed. That would be the evidence needed for the FCC to follow through with any designated fines or penalties."

There was a short silence as the Cabinet members looked over the report while listening to the president. Then Joseph Carpenter, Commerce Secretary, spoke first. "I like the general idea very much. First of all, we need some way to clamp down on those who abuse the limits. But, secondly, this proposal is a way to do it without expanding government agencies and their budgets. I am assuming I have permission to work with the FCC on the details and then bring back some final proposal for approval."

"If no one objects," Ward quickly interjected and then looked around the table, seeing heads shaking in the negative. "See that it is done. You might also make certain that the justice department is agreeable before reporting back."

"Of course," was Joseph's response.

Chapter 3:
"A Sticky Wicket"

"The next item on the agenda is in regard to what is commonly named 'gun control' by those who want no changes regarding laws related to 'Article Two' of the 'Bill Of Rights.' The exact wording of that section is also included so that we have it directly before us for this discussion. 'A well-regulated Militia, being necessary to the security of a Free State, the right of the people to keep and bear arms, shall not be infringed.'

"This issue has been severely controlled by the National Rifle Association for too many decades. It has been for so long of a time that the 'Article Two' has taken on a context which was never intended by our Founding Fathers. I have even heard of one politician who declared, 'This Second Amendment gives me the right to protect my family from anyone intending them harm.' Now, that is really a wild interpretation of what is written. It is also a dangerous one."

There was a pause in the president's presentation—enough to permit visual and some vocal agreement from those present. All of them knew enough about history—and also, recent events—that the NRA had long controlled how Congress voted on gun regulations. Because of NRA lobbying in the past—because of the huge amounts of money given to the support of both political parties—a lot of proposed legislation was delayed in committee for years, never making it to the point of presenting it for a vote.

Steve Layton of Justice was the first to be recognized by Ward. "Steve, would you give us some insight regarding this issue?"

"I'll try to be as brief as possible, but—as you all know—this is a 'loaded' issue; if you will pardon my pun." There were some laughs and also some groans. Then Steve continued. "My experience in law has taught me that there are too many lawyers who really don't know how to accurately read the English language. Long ago I had a young couple come to me to straighten out a decision made by another lawyer regarding the will of the wife's parents. That lawyer completely misread the will. In this case the wife's father had died, but his wife was yet alive. That lawyer's decision was made on the basis of the will's intention 'if both the husband and wife had died.' She did that because she did not read correctly. That is why that couple came to me. They were both correct in their own reading of the will.

"Now, I find the same thing in this gun issue. There was a purpose in the minds of those men who wrote and approved it. That purpose is plainly stated in the Second Article. It is that this new nation would have an armed force—able to handle a gun—to defend the nation from outside enemies. That is the only intention stated there. It does not define the types of weapons. It does not give permission to citizens to shoot anyone. The NRA has assumed it states all of that, and it has propagated that erroneous interpretation upon our culture. That was easy to do because we were—for many generations—a frontier nation.

"Therefore, Mr. President, I think it logical and proper that this issue ought to be taken to court to be settled. The best way is to prepare a proposed law, have it passed, and then let the NRA sue us. We have a good case, based on the vagueness of the Article. We also could muster support for the passing of such a law because of term limits and no lobbying."

"Thank you, Steve. The floor is now open for discussion."

There was no lack of people wanting to talk. It was a good discussion about the various issues involved: types of guns available, the failure of previous checks before approval for purchase, one person was very emotional about better regulation because a member of his family had been killed with an automatic gun in a restaurant. Another member commented against the concealed-carry law, saying he always wondered how the "right to bear arms" could be so interpreted as to permit that.

After three quarters of an hour, Ward ended the discussion. "I would like the justice department to be assigned to work with my chief of staff to take what has been said here and try to formulate a proposal for a bill that might be submitted to Congress—a proposal that we will give to each of you a few weeks before we will discuss it again and vote on it one way or the other. Again—especially with such a sensitive issue—there cannot be any leakage regarding this issue. I do not want this discussed in the news before we present something we agree on. If we end up not agreeing to move forward, we might then report what transpired."

The Cabinet then moved on to more perfunctory items and then adjourned.

Chapter 4:

"The End Is Near"

The president's chief of staff had a pile of papers when he entered the Oval Office for his morning meeting. Ward looked at him, smiled, and then said, "You had better sit before you drop that pile on the floor and we will have to call for help to straighten up the mess."

"Thank you, Mr. President. I'll try to be careful sitting."

"What is in that pile? Did you clean out your desk?"

"No, Sir. This all came in this morning. They are reports, e-mails, newspaper items from around the nation, and more are yet coming into the West Wing."

"What's going on?"

Ronald sat down carefully and laid the pile next to himself on the couch. "Yesterday a TV minister from Georgia announced that he has received word from God—in a vision—that God is returning to earth the end of this month to bring about the 'final judgment and destruction of this earth.'

"He has a large TV audience who are helping him by contacting as many newspapers as possible, plus saturating the network with blogs and websites and e-mails spreading that news. While this kind of thing has happened often in the past, now it is expanded to the point where this administration needs to give some clarifying response. I simply do not know what we can do."

Both Ward and his chief of staff remembered those past instances. The predictions of "The End" had become quite common during the past two or three decades, a great increase from previous times. It was as if every independent clergy wanted to get in on the publicity it generated.

"Well," Ward began, "this is not something I thought I would need to handle as president. I did give responses when I was a pastor. People did ask questions about such 'prophecies,' and I needed to tell them what I thought."

Ward picked up a few of the papers and glanced at them. He hesitated a moment and then continued. "In view of the extreme increase of this problem—it seems to have become a national problem—I think it is time for me to say something as an informed president before the trend becomes disruptive.

"When I was a pastor, I was able to give one lecture on the subject at a religion course at Penn State. It was quite an honor for me to do it, and I did months of preparation. I titled the presentation 'THE WORLD WILL END TOMORROW! THANK GOD IT IS ALWAYS TODAY!' I described the lecture as: 'an in-depth examination of issues relating to the numerous and false prophecies about the end of the world—using Scripture, History, and Reason.' Maybe it is time for me to present it again in some form."

Ronald thought for a minute. "My hesitation in responding was not because I didn't like the idea. I do. I think the situation calls for it. I was first thinking about the 'How?' of doing it."

"Well, you mentioned the present issue is spread through the internet, as well as newspaper reports. Would it work for us to do the same?"

"Of course it will. Hopefully it will even work better coming from the president. How long was your lecture?"

"It was the usual fifty minutes, but I could condense it some without damaging my argument."

"How much time do you need before we could include it on our website?"

"Because of the urgency of stopping this before it gets worse, let me check my schedule." Ward went to his desk and looked. After a minute or so, he sat back down. "It looks like we could make some changes to my schedule for tomorrow and the next day, and I could start on the revision tonight. I'll ask Lisa if she has time to make suggestions before tonight."

"When do you want me to give a press release on this?"

"I think you can do that today, mentioning that the president's response will be on our website by the end of this week. I have also thought I would use my 'fireside talk' to advertise that fact. It won't hurt to try to reach as many people as possible."

"I am certain that will be the best way to handle it. If you can find a copy of your entire lecture, I would like to have it as soon as possible. I'll have my assistant read it and give me any suggestions she can. It might be that the press will want to print the entire lecture. This is a newsworthy item."

Ward called his secretary and told him where to find the lecture in his personal computer and print three copies as soon as he could. In the interim, Ward and Ronald continued with their normal agenda for the day.

It only took Henry, Ward's secretary, about fifteen minutes to find and print the lecture. He then knocked and entered with the copies. "Thank you, Henry. I'll take one copy and you can give two to Ronald."

Chapter 5:

"...It's Always Today"

I t had been many years since Lisa had read Ward's lecture, so she decided she should read all of it again before she made suggestions for shortening. As she read, she checked sections which would not be pertinent for the website. There are always items in an hour's presentation which are more suited to hearing than to reading. In addition, such a presentation was composed with a certain amount of repetition—verbal reminders of what the audience had heard earlier, but not seen in print. Even then, it took Lisa a little over two hours to complete her review and critique.

After dinner that evening, she sat close to her husband and they went through the lecture together. There was some discussion about a few of her suggestions, so it took over an hour until they were finished.

When they were done, Ward kissed Lisa. "Thank you for your work on this. It saved me a lot of time, and it also gave me a few hours to spend with you—even though that is a part of my 'lifetime' job description. I think it important that this issue be studied in a public forum, and now I have the opportunity and the necessity to see that happen."

"It has been my pleasure, Mr. President." Lisa smiled as she gave Ward a kiss. "I know these so-called 'prophecies' have been a thorn in your side for a long time. I also agree with you that they have also been a problem for the church and this nation, so I'm happy to be a part of doing something about them."

"Well, we will see if this plan works. But, I can just hear the religious and governmental fundamentalists screaming about 'separation of church and state.'"

Lisa grabbed Ward's hand and replied, "Didn't you always argue that the Constitution does not say that?"

"The problem here is the same as the statement of 'gun control.' The Constitution does not use those words either. Unfortunately, such 'titles' seem to be much stronger in the minds of people than the original words in the

Constitution. It is often the same in many things in life. True communication is very difficult because words are symbols, and each person has a personal and different idea of what that symbol really means. It is extremely difficult to overcome that obstacle in communication. Remember what George Bernhard Shaw said about England and the United States?"

"Yes. I studied English, too," she said. "'England and the United States are the only two countries separated by a common language.'"

"I guess I have used that phrase quite a bit." Ward smiled and gave Lisa a kiss on the cheek.

"You don't get off with that little peck," Lisa said as she took his face in her hands, and she gave him a long and passionate kiss. Then she said, "I guess it is time for us to go to bed." She took his hand as she got up and pulled him up also, leading him to their bedroom.

BOOK SEVEN

Chapter 1:
"Everything is Religious"

Ward's chief of staff was waiting for him when he entered the Oval Office. "Good morning, Mr. President."

"Hello, Ron. Have you been waiting long? I don't think I'm late, unless my watch stopped."

"No, you are even early. I just wanted to sit here and gather my thoughts. There is something magical about this room—at least to me. It seems like my brain works better here."

"You may be correct about that. It may not be magic, but rather a miracle of the history of this entire building." Ward sat down across from Ronald and then continued. "Well, did you read my original?"

"Yes, and so did my wife, although I did not tell her the purpose of our meeting about it. She thinks it was just something not related to my job— something you thought I might like to read in view of the 'latest prophecy.' I hope that was permissible. She enjoyed it and said that you had her convinced. She had to change her mind about a long-time belief."

"No, that was fine to share it with her. But, more importantly, do you think it is the kind of response this president can give to the nation?"

"Well, you must know that there will be some uproar about you handling a religious issue. But, remember, the people did elect you knowing about your previous work as a pastor/priest/minister/prophet. Did I leave out anything?"

"I think you covered most of it. There are issues that were not covered in that lecture. I need to tell you about them. They have to do with the Constitution's clause concerning 'Freedom of Religion.' Scholars have examined that concept in the Constitution, especially as it relates to the meanings of the words used there. Briefly—in the vernacular—there are those who believe that it states that government must refrain from legalizing or prohibiting or supporting any religion; but, religion yet has the opportunity to involve itself with government. That is an over-simplification, but you do get the idea, don't you?"

"Yes, but I must say this is the first time I have heard such an explanation—and I like it. That concept must have been influential in your decision to run for this office. It also tells me why you want to answer this present issue. And, to set the record straight, I approve. I also think your speech to the nation needs to contain that reasoning. There will be those who would like to debate it, but your speech is your own property."

The two of them then began to list the general ideas and direction for Ward's television talk to the nation. Ronald would give those directions to the speech writer and work with him. The next item was the condensed lecture which would be posted on the presidential website. After that they each returned to their own work for the day.

Chapter 2:
"Now, Hear This!"

The countdown was ending: "Five, four, three, two, one...."

"Good evening. This is President Adamson, speaking to you from your White House." Ward had begun each TV "fireside chat" with those words. "Tonight I need to talk about what has become an increasingly serious issue in this nation. It has to do with what some religious people name as 'The Second Coming of Jesus,' or 'The End of the World,' or any number of other designations. I need to talk about it because my office received a request from the latest 'prophet of doom' to do so. However, he is not going to like what I have to say.

"But, for those who believe that religion should have no 'say' in government, let me simply tell you this. Our Constitution states that government can give no physical support to any particular religion, but it does not prohibit religion from involvement in government. It was because this latest so-called prophet chose to involve his government that I now have the right to answer him. Further, as I will remind you later, this type of religion has had bad effects in government, and I need to correct those results. What I have to say tonight will be brief, but a more detailed report will be on our website shortly after the end of this presentation. Further, if our newspapers are so inclined, there may be a copy of my complete lecture printed there.

"First, in the Bible, a prophet was not a fortune teller. Prophets were persons called by God to proclaim the words that God gave them. Because such words had future connotations, 'fortune-telling' became associated with them. But, such prophecies were always two-sided: telling what would happen if the people did not listen and what would happen if the people did listen and respond positively. In other words, the outcome was always contingent upon peoples' response.

"Next, most of these present predictions are based either on vague biblical passages or on confusing numerology in order to predict a certain date for the 'end.' Both methods are invalid, as I will show on my website.

"Third, it is obvious that today's so-called prophets don't really believe what they proclaim. If they did believe, they would give away everything they have to show their trust in their words. The only exchange of wealth comes from the transfer to the prophet from those who are sucked into their scheme.

"Finally, as I promised, such predictions have had great—even possibly disastrous—effects upon this nation and this creation. Certain government officials have argued for permitting drilling for oil in sensitive areas and even proclaimed that conservationists are wrong when they try to preserve this world because God is going to destroy it.

"At this time, I won't get into the biblical arguments. Some of them will also be put on the website. I close this part of my talk tonight by telling you this. I do not believe that God has any time or plans to destroy this creation, and I pray that God will not allow us to destroy it ourselves.

"Further, I strongly urge that no one send money to this current false prophet. After his 'day of doom' passes and he is proven to be the charlatan he is, we will file charges against him for fraud. And, no contributions to his 'cause' will be allowed to be tax deductible.

"Next on tonight's agenda…"

There were questions for the president when the telecast ended. But, Ward simply told them they could now read what he had written for the website. He did not even provide them with a copy of it, feeling it would be better if they made the effort to check it out themselves.

Chapter 3:

"The World Will End Tomorrow! Thank God It's Always Today!"

That was the title viewers of the presidential website saw. It was an immediate success as far as the number of hits. In fact, even before Ward had finished his entire TV speech, there were a huge number of hits on the site. The problem for those who did not wait was that the website was not changed until the president had finished the TV broadcast. Then, people could read:

This is a brief summation of "An in-depth examination of issues relating to the numerous and false 'prophecies' about the end of the world: using Scripture, History, and Reason." It is from a lecture given by President Adamson at Penn State University a few years ago.

"The World Will End Tomorrow! Thank God It Is Always Today!"

For centuries, people of the world have been bombarded with prophecies about the end of creation. In our own hemisphere—since the beginning of writing—we can find records of such fortune telling. Our own Native Americans spoke about the coming of the white buffalo. The Mayan culture wrote about a violent end of creation. In Europe, centuries ago, someone thought the world was going to end as the sun kept getting lower and lower in the southern sky. When it started to move upwards again, they relaxed and celebrated. The Romans even made a celebration on the day they noticed the upward progression. The Christian Church used that day (December 25) to celebrate the coming to earth of God's Son.

While I cannot speak for other religions, let me tell you that we have a great misunderstanding concerning the purpose and role of a prophet. In the Judo-Christian tradition and writings, a prophet was never a fortune teller. The role of the prophet was not to make any future, specific prediction. A prophet was called by God simply to proclaim God's Word—the Word that God would give to the chosen prophet. That was it. That was all.

The confusion comes about because that Word of God always projected into the future. It always called for human response to God's Word, and that response naturally would come after the prophet spoke. Now, there was always some response from those who heard the prophet. Some said "Yes." Some said "No." Some did not say anything; but that, in fact, was a "No."

What that means is something we have named "The Contingency Theory." What actually happened after every legitimate proclamation of every God-directed prophet was contingent upon human response to the proclaimed Word of God. Either the result was bad or it was good, all of it depending upon how the people responded. The best example of that principle can be understood if you read the book of Jonah in the Old Testament.

Judo-Christian history also adds to the problem of today. In the Old Testament, the Hebrew people did quite well for themselves. Unfortunately they began to think that they were the power behind their good fortune—not God. The time soon came when their army was being defeated in battle after battle. The leaders looked at the situation to determine the reason. They noticed that every nation that defeated them had a king. The Hebrews did not have a king—they were ruled by God-chosen judges. Therefore, they concluded they needed a king so they could be victorious again. They demanded that from God. They wore God down in their demands. God finally granted their wish. God picked Saul as King.

Actually, things did improve for the Hebrews, especially with the next two kings—David and Solomon. But when Solomon died, rivalry developed concerning the kingship and the nation split in two. Things never got better after that.

Unfortunately, they forgot their past history and began to interpret their scripture in terms of God sending a new king for their salvation. It was when Jesus refused to be the kind of King (Messiah) they wanted that he got into trouble and was killed. (I won't get into the theological part of that, except to say that the Kingship of Jesus is not of this world.)

The chief problem had been the extreme nationalism that had developed in the Hebrew nation. Having been conquered by the Greeks and now under Roman rule, the "very stones in the road" (Jesus' Palm Sunday words) "were crying out" for a military, General, King to bring political freedom. John the Baptist also preached that kind of message of destruction from God under the new king, Jesus. He even had to send his own followers to Jesus to ask if he was the one to come or if they should look for another. Jesus' answer set the record straight. Jesus was the means to a different kind of kingdom because God was a loving and caring God.

We find the most complete answer to this question in the Gospel according to St. John. This writing was done after the turn of the century by a disciple of a disciple of the original apostle. He looked back at what had happened to the Second Coming of Jesus and came to a different conclusion.

Basically, the first three gospels present the life of Jesus' suffering, death, resurrection, and gift of the Holy Spirit into one continuous and complete event. John's good news is that Jesus has returned—not as people wanted and expected, but as God determined was the best way. The Second Coming happened in the gift of the Holy Spirit. What God had promised has been fulfilled.

Unfortunately, too many read the Bible with a prejudiced mind and miss the truth. That allows people to make earthly decisions any way they want, especially in ways that benefit them personally.

In our past history we have had well over two hundred 'prophets of doom,' such as the present one. Several generations ago, there was a minister by the name of Jones who convinced his flock that Jesus was then physically coming soon. He established a colony in South America to await the day. The only thing that happened was that all the people died drinking poison.

Many years ago, a so-called "evangelical" radio minister by the name of John MacArthur wrote that the environmental movement was wrong to try to preserve the planet because "the Lord is going to destroy it."

Then there was a Secretary of the Interior under President Reagan who argued in favor of drilling for oil anywhere we wanted because we were so close to the Second Coming of Jesus and the end of the world that our drilling for oil now would not cause any lasting problem.

There was another radio eccentric named Harold Camping and his proclamation about a return of Jesus and end of the world. When it did not happen the day he predicted, he "recalculated" his mathematics and gave a new date. When that did not happen, we did not hear from him. He was probably too busy counting the contributions he had received.

There was also the "Mayan Prediction" for December 21, 2012, with its impossible "end of the world" scenario. That was never the role of the Mayan Calendar. Neither is it our purpose to concentrate on the future, other than to prepare and work to make that future better.

Footnotes:

I hope that the above brief summary will convince you of both the error of such predictions and also their danger to all of us. Personally, I do not believe God has any plans to destroy this earth. And, I also pray (and work) so that God will not allow us to destroy it.

Also, as I stated in my TV report, we will be filing a suit immediately following the predicted date—charging this "faker" with fraud. Also we will not allow a tax deduction for any financial contributions to this scheme.

Further, a copy of the original lecture has been sent to the news media. Check with them if you wish to read it in its entirety.

Chapter 4:
"The Work Is Never Done"

There had been a good outcome to Ward's speech and web report, and also a great demand for the complete lecture. It had been printed in many different forms, even though there was also a great deal of criticism from religious fundamentalists. But, basically, the people of the nation had developed enough understanding to agree with the president's arguments. That change in the population had also diminished the influence of the extreme religious right. More and more people began to "think for themselves" rather than live without questioning what they were hearing and reading.

That change was the greatest among the president's Cabinet, and it was shown immediately in the next meetings Ward had with individual Cabinet members. The first such meeting was with Commerce Secretary Joseph Carpenter and Steve Layton of Justice. The two met together with Ward because the issue was "gun control."

After the preliminary greetings, the three men sat and Steve spoke first. "As directed, my staff prepared this report for us. It contains both the legal issue regarding the Constitution and also gives suggestions for implementing a change. I believe it is the right thing to do, and I also think our suggested methods are reasonable and will eventually be effective."

There was silence as Ward and Joseph quickly read the highlights of the report. The president spoke first. "I like what you have done, Steve. I do need to ask, though, did anyone on your staff offer contrary opinions?"

"There were two people who were quite vocal about their opposition, so we had some lively discussions. I don't think we completely changed their minds about some things—especially on what public reaction might be—but our staff did come to a consensus to recommend this report to you."

Ward was interested in the objections. "What were their reasons for objecting?"

"Well, they were both avid hunters and also gun collectors. They each had at least a few of the automatic guns which would no longer be available for sale, and for which they would be unable to buy additional ammunition if this becomes law. Each also had several hand guns and the same applies there."

Ward smiled slightly and then responded. "This proves Martin Luther's axiom that 'It depends upon whose ox is being gored.' There will also be the same arguments raised by the National Rifle Association. Their 'ox will be gored' if we can get this into law.

"Our strength to get it passed is that no one in the present or future administration and Congress is dependent upon NRA support and money. In addition, I see you are only prohibiting sale of automatics and pistols—none of which should be used in hunting. I also like your method of prohibiting sale of ammunition for such armament so that eventually they will become relics when the public supply runs out. If any people want to use such guns after that, they can enlist in the armed forces. Further, we can use the argument that we made those other guns antiques and therefore more valuable for the collector. I think you have arrived at a good compromise to make our nation much safer. Thank you.

"Joseph, how do you see what we have here? Any comment?"

"Well, I know that a lot of people would not rejoice with such a law, but I think they will finally get over it. Many will rejoice—especially those who lives have been adversely affected by the weapons that are yet out there. I think we need to recommend this to the Cabinet and then to Congress for debate. I would guess that the NRA will probably sue if it becomes law, but that debate should work in our favor when the history of the gun amendment and the history of killings is presented. After all, we are supposed to govern for the welfare of the people."

"Is there anything further?" Ward questioned as he looked at both men. Seeing both heads shaking in the negative movement, he closed with a "Thanks to both of you! Steve will remain for my next meeting, but you are free to get back to your office, Joseph."

"Thank you, Mr. President. It has been a pleasure to work on this project."

After Joseph left, Ward's secretary ushered in Russell Black, head of the Federal Communication Commission. It was time to tackle the question of television.

The president rose to shake his hand. Steve did the same. Then all three sat down again as Russell open his briefcase and handed copies of his report to both Ward and Steve. "Here is the report outlining the requested work. Our discussion was quite interesting because we had never thought some changes might be possible. It's the old story of complaining to ourselves about certain things in life but never getting around to doing anything about them.

"Our proposal fairly well covers what you had outlined for us. There was total agreement with this proposal. The only big debate centered itself on two issues: one—what will be the broadcaster's response during the debate in Congress, if it becomes necessary for that to be needed; and two—how will we monitor them if this becomes law. The question about legality of such a law was mute. The FCC is designated to govern communications in this nation because it is a national item and not a state right."

Steve was quick to support that premise and then added, "If any networks want to sue us to prohibit passage and monitoring of this, they are welcome to do it. Actually, I do not see a requirement that Congress needs to act on this change."

It was Ward's turn. "I think you are correct in that, but we will inform the leaders of both Houses of our intentions. That just makes sense, especially if your proposal includes penalties for non-conformance. It might even be stronger and more enforceable if we do it that way—through Congress. I'll check with them to see if they think making it a law might be the better way. At least it would really be out in the open."

"I have no problem with that," Russell interjected, and Steve also agreed. Russell then continued with some details. "We have proposed that television programing will have an accurate starting time on both the hour and the half hour—with a fifteen second leniency for either before or after those starting and finishing times.

"Secondly, we propose a limit of six minutes of commercials for each half-hour of programing. We also specify that pop-ups are included in that time limit. We did this because that pop-up trend has continued to grow, sometimes including a stationary pop-up for an entire hour program.

"Along with that is the requirement that any writing on the screen must be large enough and remain long enough for the viewer to be able to read it.

"Our biggest concern was the monitoring of these rules. We do not have the staff anymore to be able to do much of that. I did report, Mr. President, that you indicated such a task might be done by volunteers from your wife's volunteer group."

"That is not only possible," Ward responded. "It is highly probable. The women leading that group were excited about being a part of government, even without being paid. This proposal was especially agreeable because it involved their working while they were simply doing what they normally would—watching television."

"I can believe that. That also answers what we thought might be a huge problem," Russell continued. "We did get into the issue of programing itself. Several raised the question of the use of prime time for adult shows. That trend has simply increased so that there are too many adult—specifically sexy—programs beginning even at seven o'clock in the evening. It began some time ago and then simply increased and moved into family time because no one did any regulating against it."

"The same thing is true in the history of novels," the president agreed. Most 'best sellers' are loaded with descriptive sex acts and foul language. It seems to sell, but it is creating a bad society.

"I have no problem with letting it ride—for now. It might be that we send out a letter to television networks when we complete these new rules. We can ask them to make acceptable changes regarding the 'adult' scheduling, or we may eventually have to make it for them."

"That sound reasonable to me," said Steve. Russell nodded agreement.

"Very well," said Ward. "We will present this to the Cabinet for their approval and then to the Congress. Thank you both for your work and time." The president rose, shook their hands, and ushered them to the door of the Oval Office.

His secretary then entered, telling him that Betty O'Donell was now here for her meeting about education. "We just finished. Send her in."

Betty—like the previous participants—also carried in two files and handed one to Ward. "Good morning, Mr. President. You look especially happy today."

"I guess I am. I am beginning to like this job. It gives me a greater opportunity to do some good things for our nation. Yes. So far today I am quite happy with things. I hope it continues."

"I also hope it continues," Betty responded, "especially after we talk about what I have to present to you."

"Well, then, let's get to work." Ward said, and she sat, and Ward—again— quickly surveyed what she had given him. After a couple of minutes he continued. "At first glance it seems to cover everything we talked about. But, first of all, I would like to know how things went with your staff on this matter."

"It went quite well, thank you. There were only the department heads present, but they were all interested in being involved and hopeful that we can make some great advances in education while we have a chance.

"We did include the need for at least one foreign language and also emphasized that Latin—at least one year of it—would be desirable. Following your lead, we felt there should be some form of encouragement for both schools and students who want to be involved in such a return to classical education. You will see those suggestions on page three. Generally, we will try for the foreign languages in at least the first three years of high school. Our suggested form of 'encouragement' is in terms of tax credits for the families involved and some kind of initial aid to the schools who participate.

"We think that is a better way to start, rather than simply changing a law, which could have resistance from local school boards."

She hesitated as the president's face changed to thoughtfulness. Then Ward spoke. "I had not thought completely in that direction, but I am convinced it is a better way to proceed. It will take a couple of years, but 'Rome wasn't built in day.' If it is not enough, we can try something else, hopefully before I must leave office."

"That was our thinking as well. We have seen how you do a lot of your leadership in the same fashion."

"Thanks for reminding me. Now I know you have made the correct decision. I will gladly forward it to the Cabinet. Thank you for continuing my happiness."

"We all serve at your pleasure, Mr. President—especially when it fits your personality."

The last of these meetings brought back Steve Layton from Justice. He had left the Oval Office earlier in the day for a separate meeting of his own, but then planned to return to discuss items relating to the United States legal system. Ideas had been presented shortly after the President's inauguration, but Ward knew it would take several months before any specific suggestions could be presented for further discussion. It took twelve months of preliminary talks, but the time had come to finalize it.

As the others had done, Steve arrived with copies of the preliminary proposals. Because Chief of Staff, Ronald Albright, had asked Ward if he could be present for that discussion, Ward's secretary immediately called Ron. During the minutes it took for him to arrive, Steve and the president spent those moments briefly reviewing the other proposals which were to go to the Cabinet.

Ward had left word with his secretary to send Ron in as soon as he arrived. He entered the door. "Hello, again, Mr. President." The greeting was shared by the president and Steve, and then all sat as Steve handed them their copies of his report.

"We first discussed the history of legal trials in this nation and saw how things changed over the decades. That helped convince us that many of the changes were not done for the benefit of the accused—as our constitution requires—but rather for the benefit of the lawyers. Those changes began to weaken the entire idea of 'equal justice for all' into 'more justice for those able to afford the expensive lawyers who can sway a jury to their own advantage.'

"We designated three areas which presently—we think—need to be changed. The first area has to do with juries. The Constitution states it should be a jury of the accused's 'peers.' That has now changed because of the ability of large law firms to hire consultants able to discover which people from the jury pool would be more inclined to present a verdict in agreement with their client, and which would be more inclined to oppose. We want to see a jury chosen by the judge alone, without prejudice. In addition, there is room for varying sizes of juries, depending upon the nature of the case before the court. A final suggestion has to do with jury decision not needing to be unanimous. That policy is already in place with the U.S. Supreme Court decisions." Steve paused and then asked, "I will stop with this first point. We can discuss it before we get everything confused with our other proposals."

Both Ward and Ron offered a few suggestions regarding some wording in the document. But that was all. Then Steve continued. "The next area has to do with lawyers' opening and closing statements. Through the years, lawyers began to think it was important for such soliloquies to inform jurists of some things about law. But, they slowly developed into attempts to sway the juries to points of view outside of the law. We propose that the trial begin with only instructions from the judge, and then it move directly to the calling of witnesses.

"The same would be true at the end of the trial. There would be no closing statement by either side—simply instructions from the judge regarding the duties of the jury. That change—without destroying any fairness to the trial—will greatly shorten the length of trials and increase the number of trials which can be handled in each year. What is also included in our proposal is that family members of the accused are permitted to testify only to what they know about the filed charges. There can be no emotional pleas to influence either the jury or the judge. Each case is to be decided on the basis of law—not according to 'what a good boy he has always been.'"

Both Ward and Ron smiled at that as they, again, discussed this second area of the report. Then, Steve began the final area: "The third area has to do with a recent development with our system. Several decades ago, lawyers were not allowed to have radio and TV commercials. Now they are all over the place. We did find one firm who seems to have begun it with commercials designed—in their own words—'that you may know the law!'

"Our view of that is that it was simply a scheme to inform people about how many ways there were to start lawsuits: lawsuits which would bring business to the firm which gave you the idea in the first place. Law firm advertising grew immensely after that. While law firms became wealthy and the number of firms and lawyers increased, our courts became swamped. That caused legal decision-making to draw out to months rather than days.

"Well, that is our report. There may be a lot of other things that could be changed, perhaps should be changed. After all, with the changes in electing Congress and administration, there are a lot of lawyers out there who won't be able to get elected to government positions."

Ward was almost laughing when he said, "Are there any new 'lawyer jokes' in that area?"

Steve also laughed as he responded, "Yes, but you won't hear them from me."

Then they discussed the issues a little more, made some minor changes, and the president stood. "Thank you, Steve, for all your work on this. If we can get agreement of these changes, our courts will be in much better shape. Getting 'equal justice under the law' will also mean 'speedy justice.' This administration will do its best to make that happen."

BOOK EIGHT

Chapter 1:
"A Lot on the Plate"

The following months passed quickly for everyone—especially for Ward and Lisa. Both had kept very busy in their new roles. From time to time they thought about what had happened to them the last years. Sometimes they thought about that professor in college and the class about U.S. political history.

Looking back, they agreed it was rather "prophetic" of the man to state such things about Ward—that he should think about going into politics. But, in their remembrance, the biggest surprise was the uprising of the voters. The professor had stressed that it would be necessary for voters to change the "improbable" to "possible."

Ward was nearing the end of the second year of his presidency, so the nation's accomplishment during that time kept running through his mind. Of course, he also wondered what he would be able to accomplish in the next four years and what he would be doing after that. Although he missed his pastoral work, he had begun to look at his role as president in a similar manner—being a pastor to the nation. Yet, that would finally end.

He and Lisa did reminisce from time to time. The nation had progressed a great deal under the now complete political change. Much had been accomplished by Congress under Ward's leadership. He had said as much in his last state of the nation address—complimenting members of both houses for their deep concern for the people they represented.

The nation was in a very good state. Much of that was due to the controls suggested by Ward (and people using his website) and passed by Congress. Most of the previous troubles had been caused by the fact that there had been little control over various government and social institutions and agencies. That lack had reduced efficiency and had added immense amounts of costs to government. That had been corrected—many of them due to Lisa's work with volunteers who monitored a great number of government programs. All of that was valuable in reducing the number of government employees and thus creating a surplus and reduction in costs.

The new world-wide organization could also be credited with preventing wars—thus saving huge sums of money that were now able to be used for various human aids: housing, food, employment, and health. Most of the world population was living and enjoying a much better life than ever before. Great advances in technology would increase even that in the near future.

Ward and Lisa often thanked God that they had been able to be small instruments in that better way of living in this world. It was not yet a "Garden of Eden," but it was moving in that direction as people worked with God to build a better life in a better way.

As he began—to look ahead at the next four years—Ward envisioned items for further improvement in the lives of people both in the United States of America and also in the world. It would take a lot of work—but it was "Worth the Effort."